Colt was the most blatantly masculine male Brenna had ever encountered.

His skin was bronzed from the sun, and with that chiseled face and chiseled body, he reminded her of a brave, bold hero from an old Western.

Except, she reminded herself, this man was no hero. He was a rude, arrogant man who hated children and didn't have an ounce of charity in his heart.

With her eyes still on him, and her pulse dancing in a wicked beat, she tried to ignore her reaction to him.

She knew better than to allow herself to respond or react to a man, especially this kind of man. She'd already been down that turnpike, and had nearly been killed by its curves.

Too bad his touch was sending her system into shock!

From bachelors to bridegrooms!

Dear Reader,

Our yearlong twentieth anniversary celebration continues with a spectacular lineup, starting with *Carried Away,* Silhouette Romance's first-ever two-in-one collection, featuring *New York Times* bestselling author Kasey Michaels and RITA Award-winning author Joan Hohl. In this engaging volume, mother and daughter fall for father and son!

Veteran author Tracy Sinclair provides sparks and spice as an aunt, wanting only to guarantee her nephew his privileged birthright, agrees to wed *An Eligible Stranger.* ROYALLY WED resumes with *A Royal Marriage* by rising star Cara Colter. Prince Damon Montague's heart was once as cold as his marriage bed…until his convenient bride made him wish for—and want—so much more….

To protect his ward, a gentleman guardian decides his only recourse is to make her *His Wild Young Bride.* Don't miss this dramatic VIRGIN BRIDES story from Donna Clayton. When the gavel strikes in Myrna Mackenzie's delightful miniseries THE WEDDING AUCTION, a prim schoolteacher suddenly finds herself *At the Billionaire's Bidding.* And meet the last of THE BLACKWELL BROTHERS as Sharon De Vita's cross-line series with Special Edition concludes in Romance with *The Marriage Badge.*

Next month, look for *Mercenary's Woman,* an original title from Diana Palmer that reprises her SOLDIERS OF FORTUNE miniseries. And in coming months, look for Dixie Browning and new miniseries from many of your favorite authors. It's an exciting year for Silhouette Books, and we invite you to join the celebration!

Happy reading,

Mary-Theresa Hussey

Mary-Theresa Hussey
Senior Editor

THE MARRIAGE BADGE

Sharon De Vita

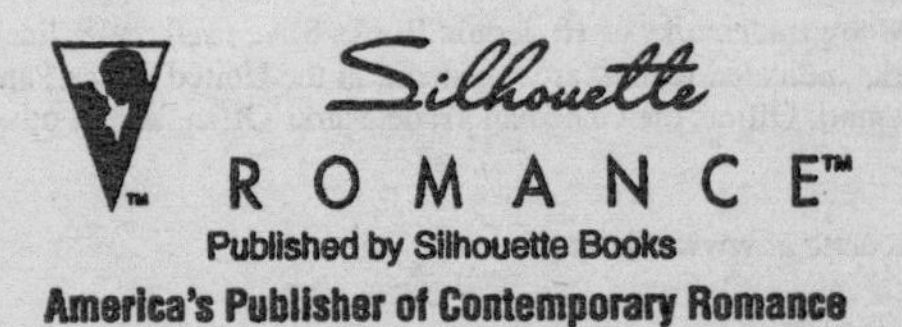

This book is dedicated with thanks, and sincere appreciation, to the entire medical staff of Hinsdale Hospital's New Day Center for all the work they do to save lives—not just of patients, but of families, as well. May you always be blessed.

SILHOUETTE BOOKS

ISBN 0-373-19443-9

THE MARRIAGE BADGE

This edition published by arrangement with Harlequin Books S.A.

Visit Silhouette at www.eHarlequin.com

Printed in U.S.A.

Books by Sharon De Vita

Silhouette Romance

Heavenly Match #475
Lady and the Legend #498
Kane and Mabel #545
Baby Makes Three #573
Sherlock's Home #593
Italian Knights #610
Sweet Adeline #693
†*On Baby Patrol* #1276
†*Baby with a Badge* #1298
†*Baby and the Officer* #1316
‡*The Marriage Badge* #1443

Silhouette Special Edition

Child of Midnight #1013
**The Lone Ranger* #1078
* *The Lady and the Sheriff* #1103
**All It Takes is Family* #1126
‡*The Marriage Basket* #1307
‡*The Marriage Promise* #1313

†Lullabies and Love
‡The Blackwell Brothers
*Silver Creek County

SHARON DE VITA

is a *USA Today* bestselling, award-winning author of numerous works of fiction and nonfiction. Her first novel won a national writing competition for Best Unpublished Romance Novel of 1985. This award-winning book, *Heavenly Match,* was subsequently published by Silhouette in 1986.

A frequent guest speaker and lecturer at conferences and seminars across the country, Sharon is currently an adjunct professor of literature and communications at a private college in the Midwest. Sharon has over one million copies of her novels in print, and her professional credentials have earned her a place in *Who's Who in American Authors, Editors and Poets* as well as the *International Who's Who of Authors.* In 1987 Sharon was the proud recipient of the *Romantic Times Magazine*'s Lifetime Achievement Award for Excellence in Writing.

IT'S OUR 20th ANNIVERSARY!

We'll be celebrating all year, Continuing with these fabulous titles, On sale in April 2000.

Romance

#1438 Carried Away
Kasey Michaels/Joan Hohl

#1439 An Eligible Stranger
Tracy Sinclair

#1440 A Royal Marriage
Cara Colter

#1441 His Wild Young Bride
Donna Clayton

#1442 At the Billionaire's Bidding
Myrna Mackenzie

#1443 The Marriage Badge
Sharon De Vita

Desire

#1285 Last Dance
Cait London

#1286 Night Music
BJ James

#1287 Seduction, Cowboy Style
Anne Marie Winston

#1288 The Barons of Texas: Jill
Fayrene Preston

#1289 Her Baby's Father
Katherine Garbera

#1290 Callan's Proposition
Barbara McCauley

Intimate Moments

#997 The Wildes of Wyoming–Hazard
Ruth Langan

#998 Daddy by Choice
Paula Detmer Riggs

#999 The Harder They Fall
Merline Lovelace

#1000 Angel Meets the Badman
Maggie Shayne

#1001 Cinderella and the Spy
Sally Tyler Hayes

#1002 Safe in His Arms
Christine Scott

Special Edition

#1315 Beginning with Baby
Christie Ridgway

#1316 The Sheik's Kidnapped Bride
Susan Mallery

#1317 Make Way for Babies!
Laurie Paige

#1318 Surprise Partners
Gina Wilkins

#1319 Her Wildest Wedding Dreams
Celeste Hamilton

#1320 Soul Mates
Carol Finch

Prologue

He'd run away.

Engulfed by fear, Emma Blackwell stood on the front porch of the rambling ranch house she shared with her husband Justin, and her three adopted sons, trying to control her emotions.

In the distance, Justin's red pickup was racing toward the house, leaving a plume of dust in his wake. She'd sent one of the ranch hands out to find him the moment she'd woken up and realized Colt, their eldest son, was gone.

"Colt ran away, didn't he?" Cutter, her middle son, old and wise beyond his years, wore a hard, sullen expression—one she hadn't seen since they'd adopted him two years ago.

"I'm not sure, sweetheart."

"Ma, if Colt doesn't come back soon, he's gonna

miss Christmas.'' Hunter, their youngest son's voice sounded clogged with tears.

''That's the point, stupid.'' Cutter flashed his younger brother a look of pure adolescent disgust. ''Colt hates Christmas. Everybody know that.''

Highly offended at being called stupid, especially since he always got A's in school, Hunter stuck his tongue out at his brother. ''I'm not stupid, booger brain.''

''Boys!'' Emma tried to make her voice stern. ''You know better than to call each other names.'' She took each of their hands, needing to hold on to them. ''We're a family, and families stick together, especially in hard times.''

Looking sheepish, Cutter scuffed his sneakered toe across the porch and glanced up at his mother. ''Sorry Ma.''

''Yeah, sorry, Ma.'' Looking guilty, Hunter glanced up at her. ''Is this hard times, Ma?''

Emma sighed. ''I think so, honey.'' She glanced at the two of them, and her heart ached just a bit more. ''Now please don't fight. I promise Colt will be home before you know it.''

''Before Christmas?'' Hunter asked hopefully, scrubbing at his itchy nose. ''It's his first Christmas with us and I bought him a present.''

''I hope so.'' Bending down, Emma gave both boys a kiss. ''Why don't you two go on in and have your breakfast? Sadie's making your favorite pancakes this morning.''

''With bacon?'' Cutter asked hopefully. ''Can we have bacon?''

''Absolutely.'' She ruffled his shock of black hair. ''Now, go on inside. When you're done with your breakfast, I'll drive you to school.'' She gave each an affectionate pat on their behinds, encouraging them to go inside.

Justin's truck had just turned the corner onto their long, winding driveway and she raced off the porch to meet him as he brought the truck to a halt and jumped out.

''Justin. Oh Justin.'' She threw herself into his waiting, open arms. ''I'm so glad you're here. Colt's gone.''

Justin held her tight, his own stomach churning with fear. ''Did the boys, Sadie or any of the ranch hands see him?''

''No.'' She shook her head, trying to blink away her tears. ''He was apparently gone before they were even up this morning.'' Emma's gaze searched her husband's. ''Do you think it was because of the Christmas tree?''

It was two weeks until Christmas, and, tonight, they had planned to decorate the huge evergreen that Justin and the ranch hands had cut down and lugged home last night.

''Now, Em. Don't blame yourself. You had no way of knowing Colt would react like this .''

''But I should have,'' she said in frustration. ''After what that child went through last Christmas it's no wonder the thought of another Christmas sent him into a panic.''

Last year at Christmas, Colt's birth mother, who could be called irresponsible at best, had gone out and left Colt and his three-year-old brother Cade alone in their apartment. Their parents had been divorced, and Colt's father had been long gone, and at eight, Colt had gotten used to looking after his baby brother.

But that night, something went horribly wrong.

There was a fire. Colt barely escaped with his life; his three-year-old brother, Cade, had perished, along with a member of the fire department. The town had grieved for the senseless death of the little boy and the fireman who'd died trying to save him.

But no one more than Colt. Although he never spoke about it, not one word, not since the night he'd arrived at their home. If someone brought up Christmas, Colt clammed up. His eyes went flat, his lips thinned and he turned away as if he'd suddenly been struck deaf.

''Don't worry, Em. We'll find him.'' Justin held her. ''Did he take anything? Extra clothes, a jacket, anything?''

Emma shook her head. ''No, I—wait.'' She pressed a hand to her pounding forehead, thinking. ''The little silver sheriff's star is gone. You know, the one he'd bought for his little brother for Christmas last year before—'' She swallowed. ''It's gone, Justin. It wasn't on his dresser this morning.''

''I think I know where he is,'' Justin said suddenly. He kissed her forehead, then headed toward his pickup. "I'll find him, honey. I promise. Go inside now, and don't worry."

His own heart was nearly tripping over itself in fear as he backed down the driveway, but he had a hunch, and Justin Blackwell always played his hunches.

"It's my fault," Colt said, his voice roughened with unshed tears. Kneeling on the cold ground in front of the little tree the town had planted in memory of his little brother and the fireman who had lost his life last year, Colt clutched the sheriff's star in his hand.

"No, son, it's not," Justin said quietly, walking up behind the little boy. Relief swept over him, nearly making his knees weak, and he placed a loving hand on his son's slender shoulder.

"He was depending on me, Dad. He always depended on me and I let him down." Wiping his nose with the back of his hand, Colt sniffled.

"No, son. That's not true." Justin went down on his haunches next to the boy. "You loved your brother, but it's not your fault he died. Sometimes things happen in life that we can't explain or have any control over."

Tears came fast and furious, and Colt struggled to swipe them away. "He was just a little kid, and I let him down."

"Colt," Justin paused, searching for the right words to ease his son's heart. "There wasn't anything you could have done. There wasn't anything *anyone* could have done."

"But I don't want him to be dead," Colt cried, throwing himself against his father.

"I know, son." Swallowing back the unshed tears in his own eyes, his heart, Justin felt as if his Adam's apple had grown to the size of a doorknob. "I know."

"And I hate Christmas!" Colt sobbed, clinging to his father. "I don't ever want to have Christmas again." It just made him think of that night. Every time he closed his eyes he could see the flames, still smell the smoke burning his eyes, his throat. "I don't want a tree, or presents or anything. Not now. Not ever."

"All right, son, if that's what you want. I understand. You don't have to have Christmas, Colt."

"You're sure?" Swiping his nose on the sleeve of his shirt, Colt hiccuped, watching his father carefully. Trust was a new emotion for him, one he still wasn't quite sure of.

"I'm sure, son." Justin tilted the boy's tear streaked chin up until their gazes met. "Have I ever lied to you?"

Colt's gaze dropped in shame. "No sir."

"Well, I'm not about to start now." Draping his arm around his son, Justin pulled him close, holding him against his warmth. He could almost feel the nine-year-old's heart breaking, finally he drew back, releasing his boy.

"Say your piece son, then let's go home. Your mother and your brothers are worried."

Justin stood up and stepped back a few steps to give the little boy privacy.

Colt looked down at the struggling seedling for a long time, saying nothing. Then he stood up, wiped his eyes with his sleeve, and turned toward his father, who was waiting quietly, his hand outstretched. Colt took his father's hand, and clung tightly, grateful for the safety and security of it. As his father led him toward the pickup Colt turned back once. He'd learned a valuable lesson, one he'd never forget.

Never again, he vowed, would he ever let down someone who was depending on him.

Never, ever again.

Chapter One

Blackwell, Texas
Twenty-five years later…

"Look lady, I don't care who you are. I told ya, *I don't do Christmas!* So take your plans and your particulars and stuff them in—hello? Hello?" Shaking his head, Sheriff Colt Blackwell slammed down the receiver with a great deal more force than necessary. "Damn! She hung up on me!" He glanced across his office at his brother Hunter. "Women," he said with a shake of his head.

"Problem?" Hunter asked mildly, leaning against the wall, and trying to hide his amusement.

"Just some overbearing, interfering busybody who thought I was going to play Santa for the Children's Home."

The nerve of the woman! It had been almost twenty-five years since anyone had even dared talk about Christmas in his presence. The mere mention of the word got his dander up simply because it brought up memories best forgotten.

Colt scowled at the phone. ''And on top of everything else, the woman was downright, unbelievable rude.''

''From where I was standing, you were being a little rude yourself,'' Hunter pointed out mildly.

''The nerve!'' Colt shook his head, ignoring his brother's comments. ''She actually hung up on me. I tell you, Hunter, there's no respect for the law anymore, no—''

''Colt?'' Hunter waited for his brother to run out of steam. ''Colt!''

Drawn out of his reverie by his brother's tone of voice, Colt frowned in confusion. ''Jeez, what?''

''That...uh...overbearing, bossy, interfering—''

''Don't forget rude—'' Colt added, making Hunter sigh.

''Yes, I heard you. That...*rude,* bossy, interfering woman wouldn't happen to be Brenna Baxter would it?''

''Brenna Baxter?'' Colt repeated in surprise, searching his memory. He wasn't even certain he gave her a chance to say her name, not that he'd even remember it. His frown deepened and he replayed their rather confrontational conversation in his mind. ''Yeah, yeah, I think that might have been her name.'' Colt glanced across the room at his brother, who looked entirely too pleased. "How the heck did you know?" he asked suspiciously, jumping to his feet. "Do you know this Baxter woman? Did you sic this chick on me?" Colt's fists clenched at his sides. Hunter might be a few inches taller, but he could still take him if need be.

"Nope." Hunter shook his head, lifting his hand in the air as a peace signal. "Not me. I know better. I've never met the woman." He grinned at the look of relief that passed over Colt's face, deliberately waiting a beat. "But you...uh...might want to talk to mom."

Colt's look of relief quickly turned to panic. There wasn't anything—not anything—either he nor his brothers wouldn't do for their mother. Or their father.

"Mom?" he repeated in shock, lifted his head to look at his brother. "Mom sicced this woman on me?"

"I believe so," Hunter admitted, making Colt groan again. "But I don't suggest you use the term...*sicced* in front of anyone of the female persuasion, especially Mom, nor if you want to keep breathing."

In spite of the fact that Colt had never stopped avoiding Christmas, their mother Emma had never stopped hoping that she'd be able to break through the self-imposed barriers he'd erected around himself each holiday season.

Colt glared at his brother. "You may be the town pediatrician, Hunter, but if you don't start giving me some answers you're going to *need* a doctor. Now fess up. What the hell is going on? And what does this Baxter chick want with me?"

"You mean besides your hide?" Trying to hide a grin, Hunter shrugged. "I don't know, like I said, you'd better talk to Mom."

"You must know something," Colt insisted.

"All I know is that Mom and Dad are on the board of the Children's Home and they've spent a lot of time raising funds to renovate the joint. Especially Mom."

Having grown up in the Children's Home, their father Justin had a soft spot for the home.

"Yeah," Colt acknowledged suspiciously. "I know that. Everyone in town knows that. So what does that have to do with me?"

"Well, I'm not sure," Hunter admitted with a frown of his own. "The renovations are supposed to start any day now so that they can be finished in time for Christmas."

"Christmas again," Colt muttered under his breath.

"In addition," Hunter went on, ignoring his brother's sarcasm, "to raising funds for the renovation, Mom and Dad had a hand in hiring the new director. She took over the home about three months ago."

It took a moment for Hunter's words to register, then realization, quickly followed by annoyance kicked in.

"Oh Lord," Colt groaned, dragging a hand

through his dark hair. "And this new director...she wouldn't by an chance be the same rude, overbearing, bossy busybody I just basically told to go take a...a flying leap?"

Hunter's grin was smug. "I believe, bro, she is one and the same." Laughing at the look on Colt's face, Hunter lifted his coffee cup in the air in a mock salute only brothers could appreciate. "Looks to me like you're between a pickle and a pork belly, Colt." Hunter sipped his coffee. "So tell me, exactly how rude were you?"

"Don't ask," Colt moaned, thinking about his rather...spirited conversation with the Baxter woman. And what his mother's reaction would be when she found out about it.

He and his brothers may be grown, but their mother still scared the living daylights out of them simply because they all loved her so fiercely they lived in dread of ever doing anything to disappoint her.

"Why me?" Colt asked, glancing skyward. "Why didn't mom sic this chick on you or Cutter?"

Hunter shook his head. "Don't get me involved in this. I've got a private practice as well as responsibility for the tribal clinic, not to mention a wife and a definitely-trying-to-be-rebellious adopted teenage son." Hunter lifted his hand in the air to ward off Colt's protest. "And don't even think about corralling Cutter. While he and Sara are home for the holidays, he's handling all the ranching duties." Their adopted brother Cutter was married to Colt's natural sister, who'd been born and then given up for adoption by their natural mother long after Colt had been taken away from his natural mother.

It had been years until Colt even knew he had a sister. It wasn't until their adopted mother, Emma, learned of Sara, that Cutter set out to find her in order to reunite Colt with the sister he'd never even known about. Cutter had not only found the woman, who'd grown up in a small Amish community in Illinois, but Cutter had fallen in love with her and married her.

Now that Cutter and Sara were married, and Sara and Colt reunited, Sara and Cutter split their time between the Blackwell ranch in Texas, and the small Amish community where Sara still taught, and where Cutter and Sara lived during the school year.

"And lest you forget, Colt, Sara's about to give birth. To twins. She's gotta take it easy until her due date, so Cutter's got his hands full." Hunter couldn't prevent a smile from sliding across his face. "So that leaves...you."

"Thanks," Colt groaned. "For leaving me holding the bag."

Hunter laughed, setting his empty cup in the sink. "That bag better be filled with toys, presents, and a very loud Ho! Ho! Ho! unless you want Mom on your case," Hunter said, reaching for his coat.

"Where are you going?" Colt asked suddenly.

"To the hospital. I've got to make rounds."

"You mean you're just going to leave me to deal with this...this...mess alone?"

"Looks that way." Hunter grinned, tucking his hands in his pocket. "See you tonight."

Colt sank back down into his chair, glaring at his brother's retreating back, wondering how he was going to get out of this mess?

Another thought followed on its heel, a thought that brought an ache to his heart; he couldn't—wouldn't—let his mother down. The mere thought brought an ache to his heart so deep he was certain he could actually feel it.

But he knew he couldn't play Santa either. No way in hell. Somehow, he'd have to come up with a solution that would satisfy everyone, and yet still give him the peace he needed to avoid his own haunting memories.

Brenna Baxter took one look at the large, obviously annoyed man pacing the wood off the long hallway outside of her office and knew he was trouble.

With a capital T.

She'd already had one go-round today with a rude, arrogant man and she wasn't in the mood put up with any more male nonsense today.

Thinking about her early morning telephone conversation with Sheriff Colt Blackwell made Brenna's famous Irish temper simmer. Again.

The man was sorely in need of a distemper shot she'd decided.

Add to that the fact that he either hated kids,

Christmas or both, and she pretty much figured she had the guy's number.

And it was definitely a wrong number, she decided, regretting even placing the call to the sheriff. If she hadn't been desperate...well, no point in ruminating about it now.

She peeked at the pacing man again and scowled, instinctively knowing he was definitely trouble. Men who looked like him usually were.

His black hair, worn longer than necessary, curled gently around the collar of his chambray shirt, which was tucked into well-worn jeans that hugged his muscled frame.

There was strength in his arms, his legs, his shoulders as well as in that incredibly chiseled face that was comprised of sharp planes and angles, and cheekbones sharp enough to carve glass.

He carried himself with a kind of arrogant insolence bolstered by that natural male self-confidence that always left her feeling slightly...addled.

Tucking back an errant lock of long auburn hair, she closed her eyes, and pushed a pile of unpaid bills to one corner of her already cluttered desk, hoping to ignore them for the moment, wishing she could as easily ignore the large man pacing outside her office as well.

Her hand froze on the pile of unpaid bills and she glanced at the man again. Mother of Mercy, she hoped he wasn't another...bill collector, coming to...collect.

Brenna gave another weary sigh. If he was, he

was going to be even more annoyed to know the Home didn't have the money to pay him for whatever services he had rendered. At least not yet.

Because of budgetary cutbacks in state funds, their operating capital had run out with a month left in the fiscal year.

The state legislature had passed an emergency bill to fund the Home until the new budget was passed, but she'd learned the government's idea of an emergency, and hers were light-years apart.

It could be weeks before she received the operating capital necessary to pay overdue bills.

Until then, she'd merely been putting off as well as avoiding as many bill collectors as she could.

But she had a feeling, the man pacing outside her office could not—would not—be avoided.

Accepting the inevitable, Brenna smoothed down the jacket of her suit, searched under her desk with one stockinged foot for her high-heeled pumps and prepared to go to battle with another man.

Again.

Like a caged animal waiting to be freed, Colt paced the length of the long, narrow hallway outside Brenna Baxter's office, wondering if the woman was deliberately keeping him waiting just to be rude.

His cowboy boots clicked softly on the faded linoleum as he glanced around the Children's Home, trying not to let the condition of the joint tug at his heartstrings.

No wonder his parents had raised funds to renovate the place. It didn't need a Santa Claus; a construction crew seemed more ideal. Old and slightly decrepit, the joint was sorely in need of renovations. A good coat of paint wouldn't hurt either.

The thought that children had to live like this riled him to no end, reminding him of his own pathetic childhood before the Blackwells took him in.

There was an anemic-looking Christmas tree sitting in one corner of the long, drafty hallway. Bare as a dog's bone, and listing slightly to the left, the tree looked like it was sorely in need of life support.

Sitting next to the tree was a water-stained brown box overflowing with an odd assortment of colorful, handmade ornaments: the kind kids made in kindergarten. A tangled pile of lights sat on the floor near the tree, right under a sorry-looking wreath, already turning brown around the edges. Overhead, the crackling sounds of a Christmas carol seeped out of an aging speaker, squeaking through the air.

The sight and sounds of Christmas immediately colored Colt's mood. He felt as if he were suffocating; the need to run as far and as fast as he could was nearly overwhelming.

But at least he'd had the presence of mind to come up with what he thought was a pretty ingenious plan, one that would hopefully get him back in everyone's good graces, especially his mother's, yet still allow him the peace he needed to retreat into his own world right now.

Still pacing, Colt nearly shivered as a gust of wind

rattled the windows. Frowning, he glanced up at the nearly floor-to-ceiling windows. They were old and ill-fitting. Clearly new windows were in order. Even Texas could get frigid in December.

Concerned, he glanced around more carefully this time. Although the structure looked sturdy, the cosmetic blights made the place look like it was in worse condition than it really was.

A sound had his head turning. Colt's interest peaked as he watched as a pair of heels—red as rubies and just as shiny—pick their way over the faded linoleum toward him.

He let his eyes quickly do a visual appraisal from the long, gorgeous legs, touching briefly on the elegant city slicker suit in a shade of Christmas red that was so eye popping, it should have been outlawed.

Colt's gaze halted and his mouth went dry. The suit clung to a body that could have been carved right out of a cowboy's fantasy.

Reluctantly, he dragged his gaze from that "sweet as sin" body, and lifted it to her face. His breath almost backed up in his lungs. Lord have mercy. She was undeniably, unbelievable...gorgeous. No doubt about it.

Her skin was as pale as the moon. Her eyes were as deep and green as a cat, and just as cool and calm. Long, auburn hair cascaded past her shoulders. Her mouth was full and heart shaped, just the kind of mouth that seemed to be begging to be kissed.

And kissed well.

The combination was an incredible mixture of head-turning beauty and mind-boggling sensuality that immediately made him relax. There wasn't a woman alive who'd ever been immune to his charm. He definitely believed in the love-'em-and-leave-'em philosophy; it made things much simpler. He didn't trust women. Period. He'd learned how devious women could be from his birth mother, and he wasn't a man who forgot a lesson.

"Ms. Baxter?" He flashed her a smile.

"*Dr.* Baxter," she corrected coolly.

"Dr?" he repeated in surprise, certain she was putting him on. He let his eyes traipse over her again. With those looks and that body, she was more likely to be the cause of a heart attack, not the *cure* for one. "And...uh...exactly what kind of doctor are you?" he asked in amusement.

Brenna blew out an exasperated breath. Another arrogant, insolent blockhead, Brenna decided with a sigh. Another man who was obviously more interested in appearance than substance. And Lord, she'd had her fair share of those kind of men.

Not at all amused by his...amusement, Brenna wondered how insolent this man would be if he knew how hard she'd worked for her degrees and all that she'd accomplished.

The years of worry, of frustration, of struggling and juggling—school, two jobs, a handicapped child, as well as a mountain of medical bills—all on her own, never having, wanting or needing anyone to depend on.

Never knowing from one month to the next if she'd be able to make ends meet or have a roof over their heads. The hand-to-mouth existence that was necessary in order to achieve her dream, to provide a secure future for herself and her daughter, Charlie.

From the moment her husband had walked out on them—three months after learning their newborn daughter would be physically handicapped and would never be accepted into his highly social, highly visible life—until this moment, everything Brenna had done she'd done on her own in an effort to secure a happy life, home and future for her daughter so that neither she nor her child would ever have to depend on anyone—especially not another man—ever, ever again.

Not for anything.

And she wasn't about to apologize or explain her actions to anyone, especially a man. Particularly *this* man.

Determined to put this man in his place, Brenna lifted her chin, trying to control her simmering temper.

"I have a Ph.D. in Social Work, as well as a Master's Degree in Early Childhood Development with a subspecialty in disabled children." Her voice had enough starch to stiffen a porcupine's spine. "And," she added, wondering why his insolent, arrogant smile had made her so defensive. "I assure you I'm more than qualified to be the director of the facility.'' Her steely gaze met his. ''Now that we've established who I am, perhaps you might be so kind as to tell me who you are? '' One delicate auburn brow arched.

''Colt Blackwell,'' he said, flashing her another charming grin as he extended his hand toward her. ''*Sheriff* Colt Blackwell.''

Chapter Two

Her gaze flew to his and Brenna merely stared at him, dumbfounded, certain she'd heard him wrong.

"E...excuse me?" She blinked. This wildly, unbelievably attractive man couldn't possibly the unbearably rude, overbearing imbecile she'd hung up on this morning.

Could it?

"Colt Blackwell," he repeated, leaning close and speaking directly into her startled face. "Sheriff Colt Blackwell. We...uh...spoke on the phone this morning, remember?"

"You!" she hissed, her temper getting the best of her. He was too close; that glorious face, those eyes, that unbelievable mouth was just too close for comfort. Stunned by her immediate reaction to him, she reared back, eyes flashing, temper simmering as reality sank in. ''You're that...that...rude, insufferable—''

He held his hands in the air. ''Whoa, whoa, whoa, now, there's no need for name calling, Doc. If I recall, you were being a little rude yourself,'' he said, wiggling his brows at her. ''You hung up on me.''

''And not a moment to soon,'' she fumed, mentally replaying their earlier conversation and growing annoyed all over again.

If he thought his too-cute-for-words act was going to get any sympathy, he would be sorely mistaken.

Her eyes frosted and her chin lifted. Attractive or not, the man was...infuriating.

''What do you want?'' she demanded, wanting to be rid of him as soon as possible. It had been a long time since the mere presence of a man, especially one who looked like him, could raise her hackles, or her pulse, and she didn't like it. Not one bit.

''Seems to me you're the one who wanted something. You called me? Remember, Doc?''

Brenna couldn't help it, she bristled. Every time he called her ''Doc,'' it sounded like a caress, which only further infuriated her.

''Unfortunately it would be difficult for me to forget.'' Her eyes darkened with temper. ''I was under the impression that you'd be willing to help the children and the home out. But obviously I was mistaken.''

''No, Doc, it's not like that. It's not that I don't want to help—''

"On the contrary, I got your message loud and clear, Sheriff, especially the part about what the children and I could do with our plans and particulars as you so...artfully put it this morning. And since I don't have a dog for you to kick, I'm afraid you've wasted your time and mine. Good day, Sheriff."

Brenna started to turn, to march away, but she turned so quickly, she stumbled, and almost lost her balance.

Luckily, Colt reached out a hand and caught her so she wouldn't topple over on her heels.

Shaken, Brenna leaned back against him for a fraction of an instant, then she froze as her breath came out on a whoosh of shock and surprise. His body was lean and hard, sculptured and molded like a bronzed statue. Feeling the length of his maleness against her made breathing difficult.

His fingers, long, lean and tanned circled her upper arm. His touch sizzled along her skin and her heart began a wicked, wild beat, nearly shocking her off her three-inch heels.

Slowly, hesitantly, she lifted her gaze to his, more shaken than she believed possible. His eyes were so dark, so blue, they were almost navy. There was a hint of mischief in there, shadowed by something she couldn't read. Determination. Desperation. She wasn't quite certain which it was.

But it touched her on some deeper level; some level she believed closed and locked from any man.

The impact of that face, and those dark, unreadable eyes, never mind his touch, was enough to shoot any woman's blood pressure up and off the charts.

She was no exception.

Steadier now, she realized he was still touching her; still holding onto her elbow. He held her firmly, yet gently, as if unwilling to let her go. Brenna tried to take a deep breath, but found her throat clogged.

He was the most blatantly masculine male she'd ever encountered. His skin was bronzed from the sun, and with that chiseled face, and chiseled body, he reminded her of a brave, bold hero from an old Western.

Except, she reminded herself, this man was no hero. He was a rude, arrogant man who hated children and didn't have an ounce of charity in his heart.

With her eyes still on him, and her pulse dancing a wicked beat, she tried to ignore her reaction to him.

She knew better than to allow herself to respond or react to a man, especially *this* kind of a man. She'd already been down that turnpike, and had been nearly killed by the curves.

Never again.

"Let me go. Please?" Her voice was absolutely cool, but shakier than she'd liked, but his touch was sending her system into shock.

"Sure you can stand on your own in those killer shoes, Doc?" He gave her heels a dismissive glance, shaking his head in clear disapproval.

Colt's flippant response revealed none of the shock he was feeling. She was close enough for him to smell her sweetly feminine scent; it was enough to draw a man in and to make him yearn for things that could only bring trouble.

And that kind of trouble a man didn't need.

Watching her, being so close to her was making something strange happen in his gut. He didn't like it. Worse, he didn't trust it.

Or women. Especially women like her. Cool, calm, collected. His real mother had been that way, too. Cool, calm, and heartless.

Regretfully, he released her, trying to forget how slender, how delicate she was under his hands; she might look cool, but he'd seen the heat, the passion in her eyes, heard it in her voice. He tried to ignore it. His mother had passion too—for the bottle, for men, for everything but her own kids.

"Look Doc, I came here to make you an offer." His voice was harsher than he'd intended, but he was feeling closed in by her nearness and everything else he was suddenly feeling. Old pain, buried emotions rose to mock him, awakened by his reaction to her, as well as the sounds and scents of Christmas.

He had to get out of here and away from her.

Now.

"What kind of an offer?" she asked, cocking her head to look at him suspiciously. "You've changed your mind about playing Santa for the children?"

"Uh...no, Doc, not a chance," he said firmly. He reached into his pocket, and thrust something at her. It was the perfect answer to his dilemma. "Here."

"What's this?" she asked with a frown.

''It's a check. Use it to pay someone else to play Santa.''

''But—''

''Look Doc, I don't have the time or the inclination for a long, drawn-out explanation.'' He wouldn't give her or anyone one anyway. He shrugged. ''You've got a problem. I've got the money to solve it.'' He shrugged dismissively. ''It's a simple as that.''

Brenna slowly lifted her gaze from the check to him. ''So you think money solves everything, then?''

''Hey, whatever works.'' He'd pay any amount not to have his own memories awakened, haunting him once again.

He glanced around. Christmas carols drifted out of the speaker overhead. The sad-looking tree in the corner, the scent of pine wafting through the air. The pile of lights tossed in a heap on the floor. Memories. Everything he saw invoked memories, memories best forgotten.

Just being here had put him on very dangerous emotional ground. He glanced at her and felt his own annoyance grow. If it wasn't for her, this wouldn't have happened.

Stricken, Brenna lifted her gaze from the check to his. Her voice was a whispered stream of hurt. ''Tell me, Sheriff—''

''Colt,'' he corrected automatically.

''Sheriff,'' she responded stubbornly, and just as

deliberately, using his title as if it were an insult. "Is it children you don't like? Christmas? Or both?"

A muscle in his cheek tensed. "I don't do Christmas, Doc, I thought I'd made that clear on the phone."

"Oh you did, Sheriff. You made that perfectly clear. If you think all these kids need is money to make their Christmas joyous, than I feel sorry for you. What these kids need is not something any amount of money can buy. Especially yours." Her smile was small, brittle. "But I'm sure someone like you would never understand that."

Any more than her ex-husband had understood that all his money couldn't make her forget or abandon her child.

But it could, her ex had decided, buy them freedom from what he'd termed the "burden" of their child. A nice facility—albeit an expensive one—where her ex wouldn't have to be embarrassed by a child born less than perfect; a child who's vision had been partially and permanently damaged by the oxygen needed to save her life after her premature birth.

A child whose legs would never quite work perfectly because of a pair of hips that had been twisted in their sockets before birth, requiring their child to wear cable-twister braces each and every day of her life.

When her husband had announced he wanted to put Charlie into a residential facility where she could get full-time care, she understood clearly and completely that her husband's request—no, it had really been a demand—was more for his comfort than their child's. *He* simply didn't want to have to deal with Charlie's problems, nor be embarrassed by her handicaps.

It was then, Brenna had finally realized what kind of man she had married.

And what a mistake she'd made.

It wasn't hard to recognize that same kind of man again. A man who thought he could use his money to make anything he wasn't interested in go away so he wouldn't have to be bothered or inconvenienced.

Like children.

Or Christmas.

Obviously Colt Blackwell thought his money could do the same. But she was far too smart to ever make the same mistake again. She would never, ever depend on another man for anything, especially when it came to her child, or the children in her care. Heartsick, Brenna glanced down at the check, then thrust it back at Colt, thumping him in the chest with it hard enough to get his attention.

"Hey, what gives, Doc?" he asked with a scowl.

She straightened her spine, eyes flashing. "Keep your money, Sheriff. Neither I nor the kids need it. I assure you we'll manage to have a very merry Christmas without you, or your money." Furious, Brenna turned on her heel prepared to march away from him again, grateful he couldn't see the tears burning her eyes.

"Hey, wait a minute, Doc," Colt said, stunned. He started to reach for her, but then jammed his hand in his pocket. "What is your problem? What about the check?" he asked, watching her storm away from him, her heels clicking softly on the faded linoleum.

"You need it far more than we do," she called over her shoulder. "I suggest you use it to get a distemper shot, *Sheriff.*"

Guilt was eating away at him like a hungry moth in a sweater factory. He'd spent most of the day trying to forget the stricken look on Brenna's face when he'd pushed the check into her hands.

It hadn't worked.

He'd paced his office in long, angry strides; he'd poured cup after cup of coffee; he'd buried himself in paperwork, then rose to pace again.

But he could still see her face, pale as porcelain, eyes too wide and too bright in that glorious face, haunting him because somehow, some way he knew he'd let her down.

As well as those kids.

He wasn't a man who thought money could make anything better, and in fact, had never used any of the Blackwell family fortune to his advantage.

Until today.

He hadn't thought about how his actions would be interpreted; he'd only thought of his own needs.

And the need to protect himself from his own memories had blinded him to what Brenna Baxter and the children needed.

He'd have had to have been an idiot not to have recognized the signs of pain, of hurt. Maybe because he knew a little bit about pain—and more importantly—a little bit about hiding it.

He'd hit some kind of sore spot with her when he'd thrust that check at her. What, he didn't know, but it was eating away at him.

Damn! How on earth had he gotten himself into this mess? Colt shook his head.

The front door of the sheriff's office opened, and Colt's young deputy Evan Ross came in, bringing a rush of cold night air with him.

"Evening, Sheriff." Evan stomped his cold feet and shivered, rubbing his hands together. "It's getting cold out there. Sure sign Christmas is coming," he said with a grin.

Christmas again. Colt wanted to howl. "You're late," he snarled. Antsy, he jumped to his feet and grabbed his keys. "I'm glad you're here, Evan. I'm going to take a spin around town, check things out."

"But I'm supposed to do the midnight check," Evan complained with a frown.

"I'll do it," Colt said in a voice that brooked no argument. He grabbed his coat and shrugged into it. "Then I'm going home for the night." He could use some down time. Maybe he'd corral his brothers and go have a beer. "Call me if anything comes up," he said as he settled his Stetson hat firmly on his head.

"Will do, boss."

Stepping outside, Colt shivered in the night's darkness, zipping his leather jacket higher. It might be Texas, but it was also December, and the temperature had dropped to a bone-chilling thirty degrees.

Colt glanced around before slipping into his squad car and starting the engine. Maybe he'd be able to get some peace if he went for a spin around the familiar town that had always been his home. The sight of the sleepy, silent town never failed to soothe him.

Home.

He'd been born in Blackwell, at least as far as he knew, but it had never become a home until Emma and Justin Blackwell had adopted him.

From the moment Justin had lifted him into his arms and carried him out of that burning building, Colt had found not just a father, but a family and a home.

Smiling at the memory, Colt pulled out of the parking lot and onto Main Street. In spite of the chilly December temperatures, he left his window open a couple of inches, savoring the fresh air after being cooped up in his office all day.

He drove up and down the familiar streets, glancing at storefronts, trying to forget Brenna Baxter's face. Her eyes; that haunting whisper in her voice.

He couldn't bear to think about her words—was it kids or Christmas he didn't like?

She'd hit low and hard, and the pain, the disappointment in himself was raw and real.

Turning onto the long, winding road that led out of town Colt realized he was heading toward the Children's Home.

It annoyed him.

But as sheriff of Blackwell, the Home was part of his terrain. He had a perfect right to drive past it, just to check things out he assured himself. He was just doing his job.

Colt frowned in the darkness, rolling the window down a bit lower. There was something else about the doc that was bothering him. Brenna Baxter looked cool, calm and classy, but when she talked about those kids, Lord, there was a passion in those glorious eyes of hers. The kind of passion a man would beg for.

It was at odds with the cool, classy, calmness of her.

His thoughts scatted as he sniffed the cool breeze that fluttered in through the open car window. His eyes narrowed, and he focused, like an animal who had caught sight of his prey.

Colt blocked everything out for an instant. His hands tightened on the steering wheel until his knuckles whitened and his stomach rolled; he knew that smell.

It was a smell he could never forget.

He rolled down his window all the way.

Smoke.

For a moment everything inside of him stilled, and he was thrown back in time, to another night when smoke dirtied the air, and flames scorched the sky.

Bile rolled in his stomach as his foot hit the accelerator, pressing it to the floor. As he got closer, he could see the smoke, white and thick billowing out the windows of the Children's Home.

"Damn!" Panic slid over him like a snake and had him reaching for his radio. "Evan," he shouted into the microphone, as soon as his deputy picked up. "Call the volunteer fire department, there's a fire somewhere in the Children's Home on the outskirts of town. Call my brothers, too. No, no, I'm not waiting. I'm going in. There are kids in there." He dropped the radio as he brought the car to a screeching halt and jumped out.

He didn't think, he didn't have time to; he merely reacted. The front door of the Home was locked, but two vicious kicks had it hanging from it's hinges.

"Doc?" he yelled. "Hey Doc?" He peeled off his jacket and covered his face. The long, narrow entry hall was rapidly filling with smoke, billowing upward, fed by the wind blowing in through the windows and the now open front door, but thankfully he could still see, but he knew it wouldn't be for long.

Quickly, he made his way down the hall, pounding and then opening doors, calling out as he did.

"Hey Doc, where are you?" He raced past her

ground floor office, noted it was dark and empty, but there was an eerie amber glow flickering in one corner, and smoke slithered from under the door.

Colt glanced up the stairs. The smoke billowed thicker in the stairwell, eerily moving upward. He couldn't see where it was coming from, but knew the fire had to be somewhere on the first floor.

If he went up; he might never be able to get back down. And neither would anyone else.

"Doc!" He fought his own panic, ignoring the sweat that pooled then dripped down his neck, his back, taking the stairs three at a time. He could hear sirens in the distance, and tried not to think of another night when he'd smelled smoke, heard sirens in a distance, and knew that he was trapped.

"Doc, it's Colt Blackwell. Where are you?" Training kept his voice cool, but his knees were knocking as he raced down the hallway, using his jacket to shield his mouth from the stinging smoke.

"Help! Help us." The children's cries were faint, propelling his feet faster down the hall. "We're in here."

"I'm coming. I'm coming. Stay where you are." He couldn't pinpoint where the fire was, or the children, so he blindly rushed down the hall, feeling, then opening each door in turn. Every empty door had his heart thumping wildly in his chest. His ears were starting to ring, and his equilibrium was starting to falter. An effect of the smoke he'd inhaled, but he couldn't stop. He had to find those kids.

Coughing now, he felt another door. The aging

wood was almost too hot to touch. With an oath and a prayer, he kicked open the door. Flames, hot and greedy leapt at him and he reared back.

Covering his eyes with his arm, Colt heard a loud crash, saw a flash of flames, and heard the kids' screams.

Huddled on the floor together, with a blanket over their heads were a couple of children. Controlling his own panic, Colt crossed the room in three strides, using his jacket and his booted foot to smother the flames that leapt wildly in his path, dancing crazily around the kids.

"Where's Doc Baxter?" he asked, lifting the two frightened children into his arms and holding them close. His own mosaic of memories had sprung to life, fueled by the fire, the flames, but he fought them back. These kids needed his calm, his strength. He couldn't panic.

"Don't cry," he soothed awkwardly, patting the kids' backs, heads, anything he could reach in order to stem their panic and reassure them they were safe. "You're going to be fine. I'm Sheriff Colt Blackwell and I'll get you out." Colt glanced around. The floor boards were already blackened. From the pattern, he figured the fire was somewhere below them, and would no doubt rise rapidly. "Where's Doc Baxter?"

A little boy dressed in mismatched pajamas with a wild mop of golden hair, and an equally colorful shiner six colors of the rainbow, pointed toward the door, swiped at his drippy nose, and snuggled closer to Colt. "She went down the hall to get the other kids."

"How many other kids are there?" Colt asked, glancing around. Smoke was quickly filling the room. In a minute, most of the fresh oxygen would be gone. He had to get them out of here.

"Four," a little girl about five, with a mop of hair the color of strawberries, and a smattering of freckles to match, paused to examine three of her skinny fingers before proudly holding them up to show him. Squinting at her fingers, she grinned, revealing a missing front tooth. Then her eyes teared, and she started to cough, snuggling closer to Colt. Instinctively, he tightened his arms around her. "We can't walk so good," she added, lifting her head to gaze soulfully into his eyes. He felt something soft and strong tug at his heart.

"You can't walk so good?" he asked, confused.

"Nope." She shook her head, sending her wild mop of red hair flying. "I don't got my braces on, and Tommy's wheelchair's over there." She glanced over her shoulder, pointing. "See?"

Colt's gaze followed her finger, and he saw the silver metal contraptions leaning against the bed and the small wheelchair sitting forlornly in the corner. But between him and the beds was a line of flames he wasn't about to cross.

"Well, you don't have to worry about walking right now." He tried to soften his voice. "I'll carry you."

"You're big." The little imp's eyes filled with

tears, either from fear, or smoke and she shuddered, her thin, fragile body shaking against him. "I'm scared. I don't like fire."

"I don't either," Colt said through gritted teeth, holding the little tyke tighter, trying to calm her. "What's your name, honey?" he whispered, holding her as tears dripped down her cheeks and off her chin.

"Charlie," she said, laying her head against his shoulder and lifting one skinny, scabbed arm to wind around his neck and hold him close. She started to cough again, alarming him.

"Colt?" Hunter's voice bellowed up the stairs.

"Where the hell are you?" His other brother, Cutter's voice bellowed up right behind Hunter's.

"Up here."

Colt held the kids close, keeping an eagle out for the sneaky flames as he heard his brothers' footsteps pounding up the stairs.

"In here," Colt called.

"How many more kids are there?" Cutter asked, bursting into the room and taking one of the kids from Colt's arms as Hunter reached for the other, stomping flames that had leapt to life. With the kids cradled in their arms, Hunter and Cutter headed toward the door.

"Four, I think." Colt glanced around, swiping at his tear-streaked eyes. "I don't know where the doc is. I've got to find her. And the rest of those kids." He heard the pounding of more feet, and knew the volunteer firemen had arrived.

"We'll be right back," Cutter said, as he and Hunter raced out the door with the crying, clinging children in tow.

"Doc?" Colt continued searching the long hallway, pounding on doors, "Hey, Doc. It's Colt Blackwell. Can you hear me?"

Where the hell was she? Battling smoke, coughing and sidestepping a line of sparks that hadn't quite ignited into a full flame yet, he ran his hand down the wood of another closed door, felt the intense heat, swore softly, then kicked the door open and jumped back as flames leapt at him.

His chambray shirt sleeve caught, and immediately went up in a flash of flames. He heard several screams as he tried to smother the fire licking up his arm.

"Sheriff." He heard Brenna scream, then felt her hands frantically hitting at his arm. "You're on fire. Oh God. You're on fire."

Nearly hysterical, she beat at him, her voice hoarse, tears streaking down her blackened face.

Colt finished smothering the fire with his other hand, then grabbed her, holding onto her.

"I'm fine. Calm down." Though his heart was racing, his voice was cool. " My brothers got the children in the other room out. How many more are there?"

Brenna stared at him, wordlessly.

"Hey Doc, you all right?" Colt asked. He gave her a shake. "Doc, stay with me here. I need your help for a minute." Terror slid down his spine. He couldn't let her pass out, fearing if she did, she might never wake up. He had no idea how much smoke she'd inhaled.

"Doc." Gently, he lifted her head until her eyes rolled, and finally opened. "Doc, we got the two kids in the other room. Just tell me how many more kids are left."

"Four," she whispered. "Just four...more. Because of the scheduled renovations, we relocated most of the children. The ones that are still here, we couldn't find homes for." She swallowed. "I tried to get them all into one room. But the fire...I...I..." She coughed violently. "I couldn't..." Dazed, she shook her head. "The fire...it just exploded out of nowhere."

Holding her, Colt glanced across the room, and saw for the first time four little kids—three boys and a little girl all somewhere between four and six, dressed in mismatched pajamas, crying quietly, their eyes wide with fear, their faces pale as new fallen snow.

Lying on the floor were a couple more pairs of metal braces. In the corner, standing like soldiers on guard stood a couple of wheelchairs. Now he understood what the little moppet-who-couldn't count meant about they couldn't walk so good, and he quickly wondered if this was the reason the kids hadn't been placed.

No one wanted them.

The thought came out of nowhere, another memory from his childhood, but Colt shook it away, determined to concentrate and not let his own memories paralyze him.

He glanced at Brenna, at her face, blackened by the smoke, at her hands burned by the flames, and saw only her heart, a heart that would sacrifice itself for a ragtag bunch of helpless handicapped children that no one else apparently wanted.

That knowledge touched and tugged at his own heart and he wondered if maybe he'd misjudged her.

A loud roar, and the screams of Brenna and the children shocked the thought away. He didn't have to see it, to know one of the floors had caved in.

"You have to get out." Frantic, he pushed Brenna toward the door, knowing his brothers would be back for the rest of the kids any minute.

"No! I can't leave. I can't leave them. I promised to take care of them."

"Doc." He took her arms, not wanting to touch or hurt her burned hands. He gave her a little shake. She was in shock, and she'd inhaled far too much smoke. "You have to get out before the whole joint blows. We'll get all the kids out."

He looked into her eyes, saw the terror there, and felt something deep low in his guts, remembering another night, another fire, when someone had made the same promise to him.

It had been hollow then—futile.

It wouldn't be now, he vowed.

"I swear we will," he said fiercely. He'd die himself before he'd leave without those kids. He looked deep in her eyes. "Listen to me, Doc. I'll get them out, but you have to go. I can't carry all of you."

"I won't...leave...them." she said, looking up at him and clinging to his shirt.

Colt held onto her. From the labored way she was breathing, and the way her eyes were rolling and her head lolling, he knew if he didn't get her out, she was going to pass out.

"Colt?" His brother's deep voice filtered through the smoke, which was billowing thicker now, whiter, hotter, so thick and hot he couldn't see. "Where are you?"

The heat was moving closer; Colt could hear the crackling as the fire swept through, devouring wood and material, feeding its insatiable appetite.

"Room across the hall." He turned his head to cough.

"Keep talking, Colt. I can't see, but I'll follow your voice."

"I got four more kids in here, " he yelled, grimacing at the pain in his voice. "I don't know if they can walk. The doc's here, too."

"I got you," Cutter said, stepping through the smoke into the room, with Hunter on his heels. Both tore across the room to grab a child in each arm. "The paramedics are here." Hefting the kids higher, Cutter paused to take a breath. "Fire department says the fire is spreading quickly, fed by this decaying wood building and the fraying electrical wires."

"We've got to get these kids out now," Hunter

ordered, stepping over a line of flames and heading out the door.

"I'm right behind you," Cutter said, crossing the room in three ground-eating strides. He glanced at Colt, and then Brenna. "Can you handle her?"

"Yeah." Colt bent and lifted Brenna's limp body in his arms just as a part of the floor collapsed, shooting flames skyward, licking at the ceiling. "Damn," he whispered, both prayer and plea, as he turned to flee.

"No. No." Brenna fought him, clutching his shirt. "The kids...I have to..."

"We've got the kids, Doc," he said, holding her tightly as he raced down thehall, sidestepping flames, and praying as he hadn't prayed since he was a child. "All of them," he assured her. "Every last one of them."

His words seemed to release her, and her eyes closed and her head lolled back against his shoulder. Colt raced toward the stairwell. The stairs slowed his movement. He couldn't see; he merely had to go down them by feel, praying.

The flight of stairs seemed to take an eternity, but he could hear the whoosh of water as the fire hoses poured water into the burning building, putting a damper on the flames.

Nearly blinded by smoke, and stumbling from fear, and fatigue, Colt stepped through the ruined front door, the one he'd kicked in only moments earlier.

Clutching Brenna tightly in his arms, the cold

night air slapped him in the face as he gratefully collapsed on his knees on the icy stiff grass.

They'd made it.

It hit him then, and his arms and legs began to tremble. His eyes closed, and he took several deep, gulping breaths of fresh air, trying to fill his lungs as well as calm his racing heart.

He couldn't resist glancing behind him. Smoke billowed ominously—impotently—as the water smothered the worst of it.

This time he'd beaten the hungry beast.

Relief flooded him and he buried his face in Brenna's hair, needing to feel safe, to feel...alive. He could feel her heart tripping against his.

"Doc?"

Her head rolled, but her eyes didn't open, and she didn't speak. She merely clung to him, her burned, blistered fingers tightening on his shirt.

He caught her close, held her tightly for a moment, letting his eyes close in stark relief. Now that they were safe—now that they were all safe, the fear came again, that God-awful, gut-wrenching fear that he'd only felt once before in his life. And hoped like hell never to feel again.

Lifting his head, Colt glanced around, saw the ambulances—three of them—and watched as the paramedics, under his brother Hunter's expertise, tended to the children.

Taking another deep breath, hoping to ease his aching lungs, Colt gently laid Brenna down on the grass, peeling off his tattered, burned shirt to cover her with it. He pushed a tangle of hair off her dirt-smudged face, gently touching her cheek. Her skin was flushed, and hot, but at least she seemed to be breathing. He blew out a deep breath, relieved.

"Doc." He lifted one of her hands, swore softly at the blistered welts. She looked totally defenseless, vulnerable, and he regretted the harsh words he'd said to her this morning. "Doc?" he whispered, stroking her cheek again.

"Let me have a look at her," Hunter said, kneeling next to Colt and nudging him out of the way.

"Is she going to be all right?" Hovering, Colt watched as Hunter gently examined her, letting his fingers run over her, listening to her chest with his stethoscope.

"I hope so," Hunter said quietly, continuing his examination, then lifting a hand to summon one of the paramedics. "She needs to be in the hospital, Colt. She's obviously suffering from smoke inhalation, and those burns..." Frowning, Hunter lifted one of her hands, turning it over to examine it closely. "We have to get these taken care of. The sooner the better."

"I'll go with her," Colt said, reluctantly letting go of Brenna's other hand as the paramedics lifted her onto a gurney to carry her to the waiting ambulance.

He walked with Brenna and his brother toward the waiting ambulance.

"Hunter, how are the kids?" Colt rubbed his arm where the skin had begun to welt and blister.

"They inhaled more smoke than healthy, but I think they're more frightened than anything else. You got here just in time, a few more minutes..." Hunter's voice trailed off and he sighed. "I'm having them all taken to Blackwell Memorial. Cutter rode with them to try to keep them calm. I'm going to want to keep them at least overnight just to keep an eye on them."

"Might as well," Colt said glancing behind him at the charred skeletal remains of the Home. The fire was almost out now. "They're not going to be able to come back here," he said in disgust.

"Colt." Hunter laid his hand on his brother's shoulder.

"You all right?" he asked quietly. Hunter's solemn gazed searched his brother's.

"Yeah. Fine." He couldn't—wouldn't—think about his own feelings, his own emotions right now. He had a feeling there'd be plenty of time later.

"How's your arm?" Hunter reached for him, but Colt shook him off.

"I'm fine, Just fine." He kept walking, bending to pick up his shirt. It had fallen off Brenna as the paramedics carried her.

"I want to check that arm," Hunter said forcefully.

"I'm fine," Colt insisted, irritated. He didn't want tending, and he didn't want mothering. Now that the terror had passed, all he wanted was a quiet corner, and a full bottle so he could drown his memories, old and new, and forget about the terror that was going to torment those kids.

Tonight and for a lot of nights to come.

"You're not fine, Colt. That arm needs medical attention." Hunter, the tallest of all three Blackwell boys was a gentle soul who had a calm, caring way with children and adults alike. He rarely pushed his size or weight around. But he did so now, bumping his chest right up against his brother to let him know he meant business. "As soon as you get to the hospital I'm checking you out."

"The hell you are." Colt didn't back down, merely stared up at his brother. His fists clenched at his sides. A good fight would do him real good right now. Frustration and fear were eating at him; he was itching to hit something—anything—just to erase the fear, the edginess that was crawling all over him. His brother would do as well as anyone.

Hunter pulled out his trump card. "It's either that," he said, falling back on the one threat that frightened the life out of any of the Blackwell men. "Or I call Mom and tell her you're hurt."

"You wouldn't dare?" A long, silent moment passed. Colt's eyes narrowed. "All right, all right," he finally snarled, blowing out an exasperated breath, knowing when he was beaten. "You win, but you play dirty." He started to climb into the ambulance beside Brenna, but paused to look back at his brother. "But if I catch you anywhere near a phone, I'm going to punch your lights out."

With a nod of acceptance, Hunter grinned. "Deal."

Chapter Three

Someone was shaking him. Colt pushed the annoying hand away. Aching and sore, all he wanted to do was sleep. At least in sleep, his memories couldn't follow.

"Colt, wake up." Hunter shook him again. "Thought you'd like to know. Dr. Baxter's finally awake. There's some guy from Children and Family Services looking for her and one of the kids is asking for you."

Rolling over on his back, Colt rubbed his eyes, then his face. He groaned, his body in full protest about being extended full length on the hard wooden bench in the visitor's waiting room for the past few hours.

"What?" Slowly, testing his body, he sat up. He felt like he'd gone ten rounds with someone—and lost every round. Stifling a yawn, Colt shook his head to shake off his grogginess. ''What did you say, Hunter?''

''Dr. Baxter's awake—''

He glanced up at his brother. ''How is she?''

'' A little groggy and disoriented. She's going be all right—in a few days. Her hands will require a few weeks to heal, but as long as we keep an eye out for infection, she should be fine. I've convinced her to stay at least overnight, but it wasn't easy. She's as stubborn as you.''

The thought made Colt grin, then he frowned, rubbing his eyes again. ''What else did you just tell me?'' He struggled to remember, wondering why a warning bell was going off in his mind. ''Who's looking for the doc?''

''Some suit from Children and Family Services.'' Hunter paused long enough to cause Colt to glance up at him, one brow raised.

''And?''

''And that's all I know.''

Colt stood up, slowly, testing his legs, almost groaning as they protested. ''What about the kids?''

''There all going to be fine. I want to keep them overnight for observation, though.'' He grinned. ''By the way, there 's one little moppet, I think her name is Charlie who's been asking for you.''

''Mop of strawberry hair, freckles to match, missing front tooth, charming as the dickens?''

''That's her.'' Hunter laid a hand on his brother's arm. ''Think you can stop in and see her? She's in the room right next to the doc's.''

"Will do," Colt said starting down the hall and trying to stifle a yawn.

"You have hair in your nose," Charlie said when he walked in, stopping him in his tracks. She was curled up in the bed, sheet pulled to her chin, fingers laced primly, eyes wide and green as saucers.

Colt couldn't help it, he started to laugh. Aching, fatigued, sore as a bug squashed under a rug, he threw back his head and laughed until his sides ached.

"Charlie, you are priceless." After ruffling her hair, he nudged her over and sat on the edge of her bed. "So, I've got hair in my nose, huh?"

She nodded, sending her mop of red hair flying. "I saw. When you picked me up. Even though I didn't have my glasses on, I could still see 'cuz you were so close."

"So you did," he said, trying not to laugh again, and feeling an enormous amount of gratitude to the little imp. "How are you feeling?" he asked, gently brushing a strand of wayward hair off her forehead.

Her eyes went wide, then her brows drew together like a long caterpillar. "I'm hungry," she complained, rubbing her tummy dramatically.

"Hungry, huh?" Some of his worry eased, if she was hungry, she had to be feeling pretty good.

"Yep. I'll bet ice cream would make me feel whole lots better." Her eyes, wide and innocent blinked up at him, making him laugh. He knew a con when he saw one.

"I don't think the doc would mind if you had some ice cream."

"Really?" Grinning, she pulled the sheet up higher under her chin and fisted it in her hands. "How's my mommy?"

"Your mommy?" he repeated quietly, wondering if he just stepped into something over his head. "*Who's* your mommy?" he asked carefully.

"My mommy's my mommy," Charlie said with a shrug of her scrawny shoulders. "Who else would be my mommy?" she asked with the practicality only a five-year-old possessed.

Colt scratched his brow, deciding he'd better try a different tactic. "Charlie, do I...know your mommy?" he asked nervously.

"Course, silly." She grinned, then frowned again. "'Cepting for she's all growed and taller, everyone says we look almost alike," she admitted, obviously quite pleased with the comparison.

"Alike," he repeated with a nod, more lost than ever. "You and your mommy look alike?"

She nodded her head vigorously.

He was absolutely certain he'd have remembered running into a toothless imp with a charming grin and a mischievous way about her. Even if she was all grown up.

"You asked me where she was?" Cocking her head, Charlie screwed up her face at him. "When you picked me up, remember?" She rolled her eyes, obviously impatient with simpleminded adults.

Colt's mind went on search, then realization

slapped him hard and fast in the face. ''The doc's your mommy?'' he asked in a voice that could best be described as shocked.

The mop of red hair bobbed up and down. ''Yep.''

''Dr. Brenna Baxter's your mother?'' he asked again, stunned. He immediately had to rethink everything he'd thought he'd figured out about the doc. She was a...mother.

He glanced down at the moppet. She was *Charlie's* mother. He had no idea why he was so surprised. Perhaps because he hadn't pictured that cool, classy lady as someone's mother.

''Course.'' The mop shook harder.

His mind was reeling. ''Charlie, are you *sure* your mommy's Dr. Brenna Baxter.''

Giggling, she gave his arm a playful punch. ''Course I'm sure.'' Her face sobered and her chin trembled. ''Is my mommy okay?'' she asked worriedly.

''The doctor said she's going to be fine.'' He stroked a hand down her tangled mane of hair. Now that he thought about it, he had to admit, Charlie did look like her mom. A smaller, cuter, less cool and calm version.

He frowned. ''Charlie, where are your glasses?''

''Dunno,'' she said with a shrug. She brightened suddenly. ''Probably on my dresser.''

''On your dresser,'' he repeated, brushing the tangled mane of wild hair out of her eyes. The kid looked like she could use a lawn mower to tame her mop. ''Back at the Home, right?''

''They got burned up, huh?'' She considered for a moment, then shrugged her skinny shoulders. ''It's okay, I guess. I hate my glasses anyway, they're ugly, and Mikey always calls me four-eyes,'' she added with a scowl.

Smothering a smile, and realizing some male-female things never changed, he patted her shoulder. ''Don't pay any attention to Mikey. We'll get you another pair.''

She brightened. ''Really?'' She bolted to her knees, bouncing in excitement. ''Can I get a pair with those sparkly diamond things on the sides?''

He laughed. ''Whatever you want.''

''I don't got a daddy,'' Charlie admitted out of the blue, glancing down at the sheet she was now pleating with her nail-bitten fingers. ''But mommy says it's okay to be just her and me 'cuz we're a family even without a daddy.''

Colt felt something constrict his heart. Fatherless children. He wondered if they ever got over the loss, the yearning. He recognized it because he, too, once yearned and longed for something he'd never had.

He ran a finger down Charlie's freckled nose, making her laugh. ''Well Charlie, sounds to me like your mommy's a pretty smart woman.''

''Course she is.'' Charlie scrubbed her nose and yawned.

''Charlie, I think you'd better get some rest.''

"Do I gotta?" Frowning with curiosity, and stalling, she lifted one of Colt's fingers and examined it, obviously fascinated by the difference in their sizes.

"Yep. You gotta." He stood up. "I'll go check on your mother and send some ice cream up." Colt glanced around the room. The other little moppet, the blond-haired boy with the shiner was curled up in his bed, thumb in his mouth, sound asleep.

"That's Tommy. He sucks his thumb." Charlie shrugged. "But he's only four. Just a baby."

"As opposed to being a grown-up like you, huh Charlie?"

"Yep," she said firmly with a shake of her head.

"So exactly how old are you?"

"I'm five years old." She held up four fingers. "Almost six."

"And a budding accountant I'm sure," he said with a grin. "All right. Time for you to get some rest." He tucked the sheet up around her.

"What about my ice cream?" she asked around a huge yawn.

Colt laughed. "I'll get right on it. But you have to promise to stay in bed." He stared down at her, worried that her braces had gone up in smoke, and not knowing if she could walk without them. "Promise?"

"Cross my heart and hope to die. Stick a needle in my eye." She made the appropriate sign across her heart, then deliberately poked herself in the eye for effect.

Impulsively, Colt leaned down and kissed her forehead. The rancid scent of smoke clung to her hair, and it made his guts clench when he remembered how close they came tonight to losing so many tonights.

Colt closed his eyes for a moment, trying to fight back his memories. He straightened.

"Colt?" she asked suddenly, reaching long, skinny arms up to wrap around his neck.

"What hon?" Her little body was trembling, and it tore at his heart.

"Can we go home? I…I don't like it here." He could hear the tears in her throat, but she was vainly trying not to cry.

"Mommy says we're gonna have a real happy—" she hiccuped "—Christmas and I want to go home so we don't miss it. If we're not there, maybe Santa won't come." Tears came, dripping down her cheeks to plop off the end of her chin. "I want to go home, please?"

Now he knew he was in over his head. The sight of tears on a female, regardless of size, scared the daylights out of him. Fumbling, he reached into his pocket for a handkerchief, then mopped up her face.

"Okay, Charlie, okay." Slightly panicked, he patted her back. "I'll make sure you can go home."

"In time for Christmas?"

"Charlie, I promise you'll be home for Christmas."

How he planned to do that, he hadn't quite figured out, but it was a minor consequence if it got her to stop crying. He could handle just about anything but a female's tears.

"Good." Giving him a smile, Charlie's eyes drooped, and she laid back down, tugging the sheet up to her chin. "Tell my mommy I love her." Her lids drooped as if someone had dropped a pebble on them.

"I'll tell her," he whispered, slipping out of the room, to check on the other four children, certain she'd be out before the door closed behind him.

Satisfied they were fine and sleeping soundly, he headed toward the doc's room, trying to figure out how he was going to keep his promise to Charlie.

He paused in the doorway of the doc's room to collect himself, then found himself frowning at what he heard. Quietly, Colt pushed open the door and stood there for a moment, listening.

"I really don't have much choice, Dr. Baxter." The man in the suit shrugged apologetically and continued. "With the home uninhabitable, I don't have any choice but to remove the children from your custody."

Unaware that Colt had stepped into the room, Brenna struggled with her frustration as well as a fresh batch of tears. "Mr. Wallace, please." She had to swallow; her throat was raw and painful. Talking took more effort than she was certain she had. She still felt woozy, and slightly out of it, but she had to keep it together; the kids were counting on her. "It's three weeks before Christmas. The Children's

Home is the only real home some of them have ever known."

Including her own daughter. Brenna felt as if she was losing everything: not just her job, but her home, her family, all the security she'd worked so hard toward for her and her daughter. The children had bonded; they'd all become a family.

"I'm sorry, Dr. Baxter. I truly am." Mr. Wallace gave her an apologetic smile. "You've done a wonderful job with the children in the three months since you've been the director, but I don't know what else to do. By morning, some of the children will be released from the hospital. Where will they go? Who will take care of them?" Pointedly, he looked at her injured hands. "You're in no condition to take care of the children, doctor. Surely even you can see that."

"Yes, but—" A coughing fit had her wincing and holding her chest.

"And then there's the matter of finding a home, Dr. Baxter," Mr. Wallace went on. "As you said, it is three weeks until Christmas. It will be difficult at best to find qualified available homes for all of them. And renovations on the Home will take longer than that I'm sure."

"You're going to..." She had to close her eyes and take a slow breath, then swallow before continuing. "You're going to split them up?" The thought horrified her, and Brenna couldn't help it, tears slipped down her cheeks. "Please, Mr. Wallace, surely there must be something you can do. Anything so you don't split the kids up. They'll be devastated." And so would she. She'd promised the kids that they'd have a wonderful Christmas, together, as a family.

For some, it was the first "family activity" or "family holiday" they'd ever had. And they'd spent weeks talking about nothing else.

Earlier tonight, before the fire, they'd spent several hours decorating their miserable little tree, as well as every room in the Home.

It wasn't perfect, but it had been magical for the kids. And that, she decided, was what Christmas and family was all about. Not how *much* you had, but being able to share whatever you had with those you loved: your family, perhaps not by blood, but by choice.

Brenna swallowed. Hard. "Mr. Wallace," she said carefully, glancing up to find Colt standing there, just inside the door watching her carefully.

In spite of her gratitude toward him for all his heroic actions tonight, she couldn't help but feel embarrassed to have him here now, as she was weepy and teary-eyed.

"Surely there must be someplace where the kids and I can stay—together—until the Home is rebuilt or repaired."

He frowned. "I'm sorry, Dr. Baxter, but I don't think there's a facility in the county large enough to take in all the children, especially on a moment's notice. And then of course, there's the matter of the funding to pay for the facility. As you know, funds from the state legislature have only just been released and it could take weeks before any money is received.'' He smiled a smile that made her realize he was truly sorry. It only made Brenna feel worse. ''And with the injuries you've sustained, Dr. Baxter, you're really not physically capable of caring for the children. I want you to take care of yourself and get well right now. Please don't worry, I'll find them all good homes.''

''Wait a minute,'' Colt said, stepping full into the room and extending his hand to the man. ''Colt Blackwell. Sheriff Colt Blackwell.''

''Sheriff.'' Mr. Wallace took his hand and shook it. ''I'm pleased to meet you.''

''Mr. Wallace, let me see if I got this right. You're going to have to remove those kids from the doc's custody, and separate them because she can't take care of them, and because you don't think there's a facility in the county that can take all of them in until the Home's rebuilt, is that right?''

''That's about right.''

Stunned by his appearance, Brenna had heard enough. She was feeling miserable enough, she didn't need this rude, arrogant man interfering and making things worse.

She couldn't remember much, fear had no doubt erased a great portion of the horror of the evening, but she did remember him showing up out of nowhere, bursting through the door, then holding her, assuring her he'd get the children out safely.

All of them.

And he had.

Her eyes slid closed for a moment and she tried to rein in the sweeping sense of relief, of gratitude she felt for him.

In spite of her personal feelings about the man she couldn't help but feel grateful. For her sake. And the children's.

But that didn't mean she wanted him poking his nose in *her* business, making it *his* business.

She had enough problems at the moment without adding him to the mix.

"Sheriff," she began, but the look he shot her snapped her mouth closed with a click.

"Colt," he corrected, shifting his gaze back to Wallace.

What on earth was he doing here? Brenna wondered in annoyance. The children were and always had been her responsibility, and she didn't need him—or any other man—no matter how helpful they were pretending to be, taking over.

In spite of the lightheadedness and the pain in her chest and her hands, Brenna struggled to sit up, determined to take control of the situation.

"Mr. Wallace, if I could find a facility that could take in all the children and Dr. Baxter, a facility that wouldn't charge the county a thing and could provide proper care and supervision, and even had a pediatrician in residence to look after the doc and the kids, would you leave the kids in the doc's care?"

"Well...yes, Sheriff," Mr. Wallace said hesitantly, obviously intrigued by the idea. "But I'd have to hear specifics, I'm sure you understand that I need to be certain that the children were properly cared for, in a proper home, with the proper supervision." Mr. Wallace looked dubious.

"Will you let the kids stay together and with the doc if I find them a home that meets all your requirements?"

"Sheriff," Brenna interjected, not certain she liked where this was going. She was more than capable of taking care of her business by herself, without this man sticking his nose where it didn't belong. "I appreciate all that you've done for me—us, but really, this isn't your problem."

"The hell it's not," he snapped. "I'm the sheriff of this county, and I'm responsible for the safety of all the residents whether you like or not, doc. So I suggest you...put a lid on it."

Her mouth snapped shut, but the look in his eyes, didn't make her resentful or angry, merely...curious.

She had a feeling Colt Blackwell was up to something—no good, no doubt. And it made her nervous. After their initial encounter, she wasn't at all certain she could trust a man like this; he'd made it clear he didn't even like kids. So what on earth was he doing?

With a sigh, Brenna realized her options were limited. Like it or not, she was going to have to hear him out.

"Sheriff, before I could agree to such an agreement, even on a limited basis, the house and the supervisory care would have to meet the stringent requirements for a temporary foster facility."

"And exactly what are the requirements?" Colt asked.

"The home must have adequate bedrooms and bathrooms in order to accommodate the number of occupants."

"It does," Colt said with a nod.

"It must also pass a rather rigid health inspection."

Colt laughed. "Now that I can guarantee." A person could eat off Sadie's floors any day of the week. And Baby, their overgrown, spoiled mutt frequently did. "What else?"

"There must be a qualified, competent adult on the premises at all times to tend to the needs of the children."

"Done." Colt jammed a hand through his hair. He didn't have a clue why he was doing this. Not a clue. Except that he'd made a promise to a little wild-haired moppet with eyes that tugged at his heart. "Anything else?"

Horace Wallace frowned. "No, I believe that's it."

"Good. Then the matter's settled."

"What's settled?" Brenna cried, still not understanding what the heck was going on.

"Be quiet," Colt said, turning to her for a moment. He saw the hope and desperation in her eyes, and deliberately ignored it. In spite of his curiosity and obvious attraction to her, he was not about to let her get to his heart. He didn't get emotionally involved with women. Period. "I'll explain later," he whispered for her ears only. He turned back to Wallace. "Got a business card on you?"

"Why yes, of course," the smaller man said, digging in his breast pocket and extracting a card.

Colt took it, scribbled an address on the back. "Here's the address of the home. I guarantee it will fit all your rigid requirements."

"Yes...well...I'll get the inspection and investigation of the temporary home rolling first thing in the morning so we can ensure a smooth transition for the children."

"Show up whenever you want. Ask for Sadie." Colt couldn't help but smile. Sadie, the Blackwell family housekeeper, was going to be thrilled to have kids underfoot and someone to fuss over and care for. "She'll see to it that you get everything you need."

"Very well, then. If it all pans out as you say, I should have a decision for you by the end of the day tomorrow."

"Today," Colt corrected, glancing at the windows where the first rays of the morning sun began to flicker.

"Yes, well, thank you, Sheriff." Mr. Wallace shook Colt's hand, then smiled at Brenna. "Please take care of yourself, dear." With that, Mr. Wallace hurried from the room, leaving Brenna staring after him.

There was silence for a long moment, before she could bring herself to look or speak at Colt.

"Sheriff," she finally said. "Do you want to tell me exactly what you think you're doing?"

"Saving your butt," he muttered, easing himself onto one corner of her bed. Even weary, disheveled, and slightly annoyed, she was still a sight to behold. It made him grin. Looking at her made him think things, want things he knew better than to be thinking. "And the name's Colt."

Brenna glared at him. Just when she was feeling weepy and grateful, the man had the power to annoy her with just a few choice words.

"Thank you, Sheriff," she said stiffly, trying to conceal her annoyance, but failing miserably. "But I don't believe I asked you to save…me or any part of my anatomy." She couldn't prevent the resentment in her voice. She'd never asked for or wanted his, or anyone else's help.

"Look Doc, I'd think you'd be grateful. I got you and the kids a reprieve." He shifted his weight on the bed, stifling another yawn.

Instantly remorseful, Brenna flushed. "I am grateful, for everything you've done. But exactly where do you think you're going to find a home that can accommodate all of us, free of charge yet."

"I don't have to find it. I live in it."

Brenna merely stared at him. Stunned. "You… you what?" Her eyes slid closed and she swallowed hard. For the second time she was certain—hopefully so—that she'd misunderstood him. "What did you just say?"

"I said I live in it," he repeated.

"Live in it?" She frowned, trying not to be terrified at the thought of living under the same roof with him. "Are you telling me that you expect me and the children to...live with you?" Her voice edged upward in shock. "You're out of your mind."

"Probably," he agreed. "But I don't see that you've got much choice in the matter." And neither did he. After the way he'd treated her this morning, guilt had been eating at him all day. This was his own way of easing his conscience.

He wasn't doing this for her, or the children, he told himself. He was doing it merely to ease his own conscience.

His mother had counted on him, and although for the first time in his life he couldn't do what his mother expected, he'd done what he could.

It was his own way of not letting his mother down.

He thought of Charlie. He wasn't about to let her down either.

"It's absolutely out of the question." Brenna pulled the covers up until they reached her chin. "I can't live with you." She gave him a look that made him feel as if he'd just slithered into the room. On his belly. If he wasn't so tired, he would have found it amusing. "I don't even know you."

"What you mean is that you don't even like me,

isn't that it, Doc?'' He couldn't help the grin that slid across his face when she blushed.

''Well, there is that,'' she admitted dully.

''So what else do you need to know about me, Doc?''

''You mean besides the fact that you don't like Christmas, you don't like kids, and you especially don't like Santa?''

He shrugged, not willing to admit or deny her claims. Either would require an explanation, something he wasn't willing to give. To her. To anyone.

''Here's everything you need to know in a nutshell. I'm the sheriff of Blackwell, duly elected four months ago. I was adopted at eight by Justin and Emma Blackwell, along with my two brothers Cutter and Hunter. Hunter was the doc who tended to your burns.'' He nodded toward her hands. ''My parents retired to Florida two years ago after my dad had a mild heart attack. In addition to my family, I've got a mutt the size of a mule named Baby, and a cranky, crotchety housekeeper named Sadie who's going to give old Wallace a run for his money.''

''Sadie?'' she said, grinning.

''Oh yeah,'' Colt said with a chuckle. ''I just hope he doesn't ask her about her sanitary conditions in the house. She's liable to bean him with a cast-iron frying pan. It's going to be a sight to behold,'' he assured her, wiggling his brows. ''Well worth the admission price.''

''Sheriff—''

"The name's Colt," he snapped in annoyance. "C-O-L-T, please use it."

She sighed. "All right, Colt. Please don't think I'm not grateful and appreciative, but you have to understand, I simply can't just come and live with you. It's…it's out of the question. I'm sorry," she said. "I simply can't accept."

"Suit yourself, Doc," he said, getting to his feet. "But the way I figure, you got two choices. You either come stay at the Blackwell ranch until we can figure out another plan."

"Or?" One elegant auburn brow arched.

"Or you lose custody of those kids." He cocked his head and grinned. "So, Doc, tell me, what's it going to be?"

Chapter Four

"This is ridiculous," Brenna said, nervously pacing the length of her hospital room, watching with a scowl as Colt packed her few belongings into the suitcase he'd loaned her. "Utterly ridiculous."

"So you've told me." Colt looked up. "For about the eighteenth time since I arrived this morning. Not to mention the hundred other times you've mentioned it during the past four days since the fire."

"And I'm perfectly capable of packing my own belongings," Brenna said crossly, glaring at him as he folded a delicate wisp of panties in a shocking shade of lime into her suitcase. Sadie, his housekeeper, had sent over a "care package" of incredibly feminine goodies to cheer her up.

"Not a chance," Colt replied with a grin. "You know what Hunter said. You're to do nothing until those hands heal," he said, shutting the suitcase.

"Besides, I'm no fool. We're going to do exactly as Hunter says. He's the doc, remember? I may be older, but he's bigger, not to mention smarter."

"Well, I don't know about that." Brenna flushed as he stared at her, a surprising grin on his face. "I mean...you seem to be able to hold your own with all your brothers," she stammered stiffly, embarrassed by her immediate defense of him.

"Yeah, well, Hunter always was the brains." He snapped the lock on the suitcase with a decided click. "It drove me crazy when I was a kid."

"And Cutter?" she asked.

Colt thought about it for a moment, before lifting the suitcase off the bed and setting it on the floor. "The brawn," he admittedly with a nod. "Definitely."

"And what about you?" she asked curiously, cocking her head to look at him.

"Me?" He laughed. "I was always all flash and lots of charm."

"Now there's a comforting thought," she murmured crossly, continuing her pacing. "Certainly something to be proud of." Colt Blackwell *was* all flash and charm, but the past four days, she'd learned he was also a lot more.

He was kind and caring, as well as incredibly giving and generous. He'd been there every day to see her.

During the days since the fire, Colt had completely shattered her previous misconceptions about him. In spite of his apparent desire to make her believe he disliked children, he'd taken her kids under his wing, and taken care of them in a way that made her feel truly grateful, and she was trying desperately not to be impressed by everything he'd done.

But in spite of everything, she was still irked by the way Colt had swept into her life and seemed to have taken charge. Somewhere along the line, from the moment she'd met him, her life seemed to have slipped out of her control and into his. She didn't like it. At all. And she certainly didn't like *needing* him. Which, in spite of her own feelings, she realized she did, at least temporarily. Not just her, but the kids as well.

Until the home was repaired and renovated, until she was healthy and fully on her feet, she had no choice but to lean on Colt, to allow herself to need him, to let him help her in order to keep and help the children.

She supposed the end justified the means, but it still left her feeling edgy and off balance. As did he, since she simply couldn't fathom the ridiculous reaction she seemed to continually have toward him.

"You know, Doc, it seems to me that you need to relax a bit. Cut yourself some slack." He stepped around the suitcase. "You've been through a lot the past few days."

"So have the children," she responded stiffly.

"Well, for the moment at least, everything's under control, so I don't see the need for your worry," he said, watching her pace the length of the room.

In spite of his resolve to stay uninvolved, and detached, he couldn't say that he'd been too effective. She'd been getting to him. He couldn't help but feel dual tugs of emotion and attraction whenever he was near her.

Worse, he found himself thinking about her, worrying about her and the kids when he wasn't with them. If he didn't know better, he'd think he was feeling downright possessive not to mention protective about the doc and the kids.

It was so ridiculous, it was starting to annoy the heck out of him. He never mooned over a woman—any woman. It was dangerous ground. He'd always been so careful to keep them at bay, that now, with her, he found himself having a difficult time, and he didn't like it.

But it was just circumstances, he'd assured himself.

Once he had her out of the hospital, and comfortably ensconced under Sadie's protective wings, things would settle down, and he could go back to the normalcy of his own life and forget he'd ever met the doc, or her adorable troop of ragtag moppets, who had somehow, in four days managed to snag his wary, scarred heart with their antics.

"I don't mean to seem ungrateful. It's just...just..." Brenna started to push her hair off her face, then remembered her bandaged hands, and scowled in frustration.

"Yeah," he said with a grin. "I know. You don't like depending on anyone. Especially me, right?" He was surprised to find that it hurt. Just a bit.

"I do appreciate everything you've done for me—for us. I really do. It's just there's so much to be done, and not much time to do it."

"Like what?" He was watching her carefully, trying to figure out exactly what it was about her that drew him like a magnet.

Brenna sighed. "It's three weeks until Christmas and this is not exactly the Christmas I—or the children—had planned. I mean, we don't even have a home, and there's so much more left to do, especially now."

"Brenna, you do have a home," he corrected quietly, deliberately ignoring the subject of Christmas and watching her try to contain her tears. "And so do the kids. All of them," he added firmly. "As long as you need it. That's not a problem you have to worry about." He flashed her a grin. "You'll have to do better than that."

He knew all too well how frightening it was to believe you didn't have a home, or a place you belonged at any time of the year. Regardless of your age, the instinct to feel like you belonged somewhere was just natural. It had been years since he'd felt that way, but it wasn't a feeling easily forgotten.

"Sheriff—"

"Colt," he corrected with a sigh, wondering why she had such a hard time using his first name.

"Colt." Brenna had to swallow. Using his first name seemed far too intimate, and she was struggling to keep him at bay. "I appreciate all that you, your brothers, your entire family has done for us, but, we can't stay with you forever. And there are so many other things that need taking care of."

"All right," he said, dragging his hand through his hair. "If you insist on worrying, we might as take the list one thing at a time."

Brenna sighed. The list had just seemed to keep growing in her mind the past four days, making her more anxious.

"When the fire broke out, the children were all getting ready for bed, or in bed. That means their braces were off, or their wheelchairs were put away for the night." She looked at him, wishing she didn't feel as if she were drowning, and he was captaining the only life boat in sight. "It's very important to me—and to the kids—that they don't lose the struggling bit of independence they've gained. Their chairs, and their braces give them mobility, a sense of worth and self-esteem so that they can do things on their own, so that they can be independent and feel as normal as possible." Tears welled, and her voice broke off. "They've worked so hard—"

"Doc." He lifted her chin so she was forced to look at him. "You forget, my brother Hunter's a pediatrician and works in this hospital. So he has access to all sorts of medical paraphernalia."

Her gaze searched his. "What are you saying?"

"I'm saying, the kids, all of them, have the chairs, the leg braces, or anything else they need."

Stunned, she just kept staring at him. "But...but

how? I mean...you don't even know who needs what.''

He leaned his face close and pressed his nose to hers, nearly startling her out of her shoes.

''Doc, I know you may think I'm an idiot, but that doesn't mean I *am* an idiot. The kids all have medical records.''

She opened her mouth, but he quickly lifted a hand in the air to stop her.

''No, not the ones you kept at the Home, they're gone, burned in the fire, but the originals Wallace keeps at the county. Hunter and I went to see him the other day. Wallace let us make copies.'' He shrugged as if it were no big deal. ''Then we went on a scavenger hunt through the hospital. Every one of the kids has whatever they need, whether it be a wheelchair, leg braces, a prescription, or in Mikey, now known as Mikey the Mischief Maker's case, a frog and two goldfish.''

She merely blinked up at him, trying to comprehend everything he'd told her. But he was so close, and he was touching her, muddling her mind.

She shook her head to clear it, trying to ignore the fact that his touch was making her feel as if she was standing in a pool of water while touching a live wire.

''You...you bought Mikey a frog and two goldfish?'' It was inane considering everything else he'd told her, but it was the only thing her mind could focus on at the moment, so she seized it.

''And a hamster,'' Colt added with a wicked grin.

"Although he told me not to tell you since you said he couldn't have anymore pets. And we can't tell Sadie," Colt added in a conspiratorial whisper. "We definitely cannot tell Sadie. Or we'll all be sleeping in the dog house. And Baby's too big to share."

One auburn brow rose and Brenna fought back a smile, incredibly touched in spite of her reservations. "Baby?"

Colt grinned. "She's the small horse masquerading as a dog I told you about. She's also a big baby, afraid of her own shadow, hence, the name. The moment she laid eyes on the kids, especially Charlie, it was love at first sight."

"Charlie?" Unconsciously, Brenna laid a bandaged hand on his chest, her eyes welling at the mention of her daughter. She could feel the steady beat of his heart, and somehow found it comforting. "How is she, Colt?" Her worried gaze searched his. "I've never been away from her before, not even for a night, not even when she was a newborn and spent so many long months in the hospital."

"Stop worrying, Doc. I told you Charlie's fine. Actually, she's magnificent. And she's a wicked checker player, even if she does cheat."

"My daughter is not a cheat," she said indignantly, knowing it was a bold-faced lie.

Shaking his head, he laughed. "The kid's a world-class cheat," he corrected. "She's beaten me every night this week." His gaze searched hers and he gave her shoulder a gently squeeze of reassurance. "She misses you desperately," he added quietly. "But she's fine, really. Everyone has everything they need—at least for now. Next problem?"

Touched beyond measure, Brenna was too stunned to say anything; she merely kept staring at him. "I don't know what to say."

"That's a relief," he said with a quick grin. "If you don't know what to say, then you can't insult me, or call me names."

Indignant again, her eyes flashed. "I have never—"

"Yes, you have," he corrected with a lift of his eyebrow. "That day on the phone. That day at the Home." His grin gentled into a soft smile. "You've been through a lot, Doc, I think it's about time you cut yourself some slack. You need to rest and recover so that you can get your strength back. You're no good to those kids if you're not healthy."

"You're right," she admitted with a nod of her head, wishing he wasn't quite so close. He was making her incredibly nervous with his maleness.

"So does that mean you'll stop worrying?" She still looked far too pale and fragile for his peace of mind. Her initial cool and calm seemed to have deserted her, letting him see the very real, very vulnerable, frightened woman beneath the surface.

She was touching that place in his heart he thought he'd closed off to women years ago, when he realized you couldn't trust them. Ever. Any of them. Especially the cool, calm ones. But somehow she'd managed to wiggle her way in and he feared she was beginning to carve out a spot for herself.

First the kids, he thought in disgust. Now her. He was going to have to put a stop to this. Absolutely. He could not, and would not, allow any woman to get to him. He'd learned early in life never to trust women. And it wasn't a lesson he was likely to forget.

"Colt."

The fact that she'd willingly used his first name had his gaze going to hers in surprise. He saw the softness in her eyes and felt a tug deep in his wary heart.

Lifting her hand from his chest to his shoulder, she stood on tiptoe and kissed his cheek, taking him by surprise. Instinctively, his arms slid around her waist, reminding him again how fragile and delicate she was.

"Thank you," she whispered. "Thank you for everything you've done, for me, and my children." She drew back to look at him, a soft smile on her beautiful face. "I'm sorry I've been such a crab. I'll try to stop worrying. I promise. At least for the moment," she added.

She was so close, he thought. Too close. Too tempting. His fingers tightened on her waist, slowly drawing her body closer. He'd been wondering and wanting for days now, actually, from the moment he'd laid eyes on her, and he wasn't a man who wanted patiently.

He dipped his head, coming closer, watching as those gorgeous green eyes widened in silent, fearful alarm as her pulse and heartbeat quickened to a frantic beat.

"Colt, I don't think—"

"Good," he murmured, brushing his lips softly, gently against hers in a whisper of a kiss, making her eyes slide close and a groan of pleasure escape. The sound was soft, sexy and had the effect of an aphrodisiac on him. "I always thought thinking was a nasty habit anyway," he murmured, dipping his head closer.

The warmth of his breath caused her lips to part and he took full advantage, taking her mouth fully as his lips covered hers.

A riot started inside of him. He'd kissed perhaps hundreds of women over the years, but none had ever devastated his mind, his heart, his body with just one touch of their lips the way Brenna had.

She tasted of innocence, of desire, of love and goodness, all the things he'd long stopped believing in, at least where a woman was concerned.

But now, he found himself…wanting to believe.

He wanted to both ravage and savor, to protect and to treasure, to indulge the feelings that were kicking him in the head, drowning out all reason, all thought, except the woman in his arms, and the feelings she'd aroused.

Aroused. He could feel his blood thicken and pool, feel himself pulling her closer to try to ease the ache of masculine desire that had flared almost out of control the moment he'd touched his lips to hers.

One kiss had knocked him silly, drowning out all reason, all sanity, so all he could do was feel and want.

She moaned again, her mouth parting slightly, and he took full advantage, letting his tongue snake out to trace the shape of her mouth, before dipping inside to taste, to plunder, to posses, to claim.

It wasn't enough. He had a frightening feeling it would never be enough. He wanted more, more of her, more of this wonderful, shocking heat that drew him as carelessly as a moth of the flame.

Shocked, Brenna's eyes slid closed and she leaned against him, fearing her legs would give out if she didn't. The world tilted, spun, and just kept going, making her dizzy, breathless.

She meant to push him away; she was certain of it, but instead, she pulled him closer, leaning into him and the wonderful feelings that weakened her limbs, making her feel lethargic and feminine and needy. Oh so needy.

Not emotionally this time, but physically. And it frightened her far more than any emotional need, for she'd never experienced this intense physical need before, had no idea how to judge or gauge it. Worse, had no idea just how dangerous it could be.

Her blood warmed, heated, threatened to boil over, clouding all thought, all reason, allowing only feelings. Glorious, wondrous feelings she'd never felt, never experienced before.

But she wanted to experience them now. All of them.

On tiptoe now, Brenna slid her other arm around Colt, pulling that hard, masculine body against her, wanting to savor the moment, the feelings this man had aroused in her. Her breasts ached, her nipples had gone hard, and restlessly she moved against him, wanting to ease the ache, wanting to fulfill the wondrous desire that was streaking through her with the speed of lightening.

So many feelings, so many sensations. Yes, she'd been married, and had a child, but she'd never, ever felt this before. She'd always thought there was something wrong with her, something lacking that she'd never felt even a glimmer of desire for her husband. Then, there had been nothing but coldness and fear because of his cruelty.

With Colt, the heat was intense enough to melt her mind and her reserve.

Now she knew there was nothing wrong with her. She was gloriously, wonderfully alive and feminine, and fully capable of all the incredibly feelings a woman was supposed to feel.

Unfortunately, the knowledge came, and with it incredibly fear, for the newly awakened feelings were with the wrong man.

She couldn't be swept aware by his kindness, or his supposed caring. She had no way of knowing if he was as genuinely sweet and caring as he appeared.

Or if, like her ex-husband, it was all just pretense. Doing things merely to impress others, to make himself seem important and caring in order to fool and woo her, with no genuine feelings or intentions behind it.

Her child—all the children—could get hurt. And she'd vowed never, ever to let anyone hurt her child, or any of the kids in her care as long as there was a breath left in her body.

This couldn't happen, not now, not ever. Not with this man. No matter how much passion crackled between them. No matter how much she longed to just lean into him and allow the kiss to continue.

"No," she murmured, desperately forcing herself to pull back from his kiss.

Shaky, she would have collapsed had he not kept his arms around her.

"Easy," Colt murmured, sounding just as stunned and staggered.

"What..." She had to swallow. Her throat was so dry, so constricted she couldn't get the words out. "What...what was that?" she asked, meeting his stunned gaze.

"Nothing," he said firmly, dragging a shaky hand through his hair. "Absolutely nothing."

"G...good. Because that...that...*nothing* can't ever happen again." She shook her head, but it did little to clear it. Her blood still hadn't cooled, nor had her heart or pulse settled.

"Agreed," Colt said. "That can't happen ever, ever again," he whispered, sliding his arms around her waist again and drawing her close.

"You're right," she said, tilted her mouth up and letting her eyes drift close as he lowered his mouth to hers once again. "Not ever again," she whispered breathlessly against his lips, lifting both arms to wrap around him and drawn him closer.

"Colt?" They jumped apart like guilty children when Hunter pushed the door open. "How's my patient this morning?" Hunter asked with a smile as his curious gaze went from one to the other. After giving Colt a look, Hunter turned to Brenna. "Are you all right?" he asked with some concern.

Barely able to drag her gaze from Colt's she nodded slowly, wishing someone would stop the world from spinning. "Yes. Fine." She swallowed, trying to gather her composure. "Just...fine." As long as she didn't look at Colt. Or touch him. And Lord, she'd never wanted to do anything so badly.

Puzzled, Hunter looked at her carefully. "Are you sure?"

She couldn't speak, only nodded, licking her lips, tasting Colt. It sent her pulse into overdrive again.

"So are you ready to go home, then?"

"More than ready." Still trembling, she flashed him a small, shaky smile, deliberately ignoring Colt and what had just happened between them.

"I feel...perfectly...uh..." She had to swallow again, then glared at Colt as he grinned, obviously pleased as punch with himself. "Fine, Hunter." She gave her hair an indignant toss, lifting an injured hand to her frantic heart. "Absolutely fine. Thank you."

Hunter patted the back of the wheelchair. "Good. But just the same..."

"Oh please, don't tell me I have to leave in that?" The last thing she needed was to feel more helpless.

"Hospital policy," Hunter said as she scowled deeply at the chair. "Sorry."

"Come on, Doc," Colt said, taking her by the elbow and helping her into the chair. "The sooner you get in, the sooner we get out. And," he added, leaning down to whisper in her ear, making her shiver as his warm breath fanned her cheek. "If you don't stop harping, I'm not going to show you your surprise."

"Surprise?" Brenna looked up at him in alarm, pressing a hand to her still pounding heart. "I think I've had more than my fair share of surprises for one day."

"Chicken," Colt said with as chuckle as he grabbed her suitcase and followed her out the door.

Chapter Five

"So Mommy, how do you like my new glasses?" Grinning hugely, Charlie preened in front of the mirror. "Colt helped me pick them out."

"He did huh? Remind me to...thank him." As soon as her hands healed, she was going to strangle him, she decided.

Turning toward her mother who was sitting on the bed, Charlie remarked, "Colt said you was gonna be real surprised."

"Well," Brenna said, trying to smother a smile and be diplomatic. "I am that. Surprised," she added with a nod, examining the glasses again. "Very surprised. That's...a...very interesting color, honey."

Charlie bounded onto the bed nearly toppling her mother. "It's called Right As Red." She kept bouncing on her knees, wrinkling the bedspread.

"Uh Charlie," Colt said from the doorway, his eyes dancing wickedly. "That's *Riotous* Red."

"That's what I said," Charlie insisted, glancing at him over her shoulder before turning back to her mother. "Colt said they're called right-as-red 'cuz they're so bright they could start a riot."

"They are...that," Brenna said mildly, yearning to stroke a hand down Charlie's wayward mane. But with her bandaged hands, she didn't dare. "And uh...what are those...sparkly things dancing up and down the stems?" Brenna asked, peering closer at the glasses.

"Diamonds." Charlie turned her head this way and that so her mother could see the sparkly things ran up and down each side of her new glasses. "Colt said they was real honest-to-goodness fake diamonds. Aren't they pretty?" Charlie stopped bouncing long enough to reverently run her finger over the precious jewels, obviously thrilled.

"Real honest-to-goodness fake diamonds, huh?" Brenna's gaze shifted to Colt's and in spite of her wariness and annoyance at the man, she couldn't help but feel a warmth of gratitude.

She couldn't remember when Charlie had been so animated or excited about anything.

"Yep." Charlie continued to bounce on her knees. "And guess what else?"

"Oh Lord," Brenna muttered, slanting a glance at Colt. "I can't...possibly imagine what else."

Charlie giggled. "That's what Colt said. He said you wouldn't ever be able to guess what else."

"So why don't you tell me sweetheart?" Using her arms, Brenna tumbled her child into her lap, cradling her close, burying her face in Charlie's wayward carrot-colored mane, inhaling deeply of her little-girl scent. She'd missed her so much.

"I gots nail polish to match. See." Charlie held out two little hands for Brenna to examine. Brenna tried not to gape.

"*Red* nail polish?" Her voice squeaked upward in shock, and her gaze went to Colt's. Maybe she wouldn't wait until her hands healed to strangle him. Red was suddenly Charlie's favorite color. The brighter, the gaudier, the better. Especially if it was something she could wear or display on her body.

"Charlie, you know we've talked about this red nail polish business before, honey, and you're too young—"

"Charlie," Colt said. "Tell your mother the rest of it."

Charlie scowled. "Oh that. Do I gotta?" she asked pleadingly.

"Absolutely," he said, hiding a grin.

"All right." Charlie sighed heavily, turning back to her mother. "Colt said I could get red nail polish only if I promised to stop chewing my nails." As she spoke, one hand went to her mouth and she started nibbling on her nails, only to have Colt take her hand, and hold it, giving her a look.

"I see." Brenna decided she was not going to be impressed by Colt's apparent finesse with her child, not to mention his apparent child psychology. She'd been trying to get her daughter to stop biting her nails almost since birth.

"And I haven't been biting 'em. Look." Extracting her hand from Colt, Charlie held them out for her mother's inspection. "They're growing. Some," she added with a frown.

Brenna took her daughter's hand and pretended to be intensely interested in the new nail growth. "That's...wonderful, sweetheart." Brenna beamed at her daughter. "I'm very proud of you."

"Now tell her the rest," Colt prompted.

Charlie rolled her eyes again. "And if I don't stop biting my nails, then I gots to give back the nail polish."

"Very good," Colt said, ruffling her hair, mussing it further. "You did that very well." He grinned down at the pint-size urchin who'd managed to charm and captivate him in a very short span of time.

First the kid, then the mother, he thought, glancing at Brenna. He didn't like the way he reacted to either mother or child. Jeez, maybe he was getting old. Or soft. Just another reason to keep his distance. Now that Brenna and the kids were settled in, he was planning on being scarce. After what happened between them this morning, he knew he had to keep his distance, since he clearly wasn't going to be able to keep his hands off of Brenna.

Or his heart clear of her.

They were getting to him, getting to places he'd sealed off years ago. And his motto was, when in doubt, particularly where a woman was concerned, run.

''And guess what else?'' Charlie asked, her face lit up like a Christmas tree.

''There's more?'' Brenna said with a lift of her brow.

''Lots more,'' Charlie said, bouncing out of her mother's lap so she could see herself in the mirror. ''Colt said he'd teach me how to ride a horse.''

''What!''

''But only if you say okay, Ma.'' She dropped her hands to her mother's shoulders, then turned pleading eyes on her. ''It is okay, Ma, isn't it?'' Charlie gently shook her mother's shoulders. ''Isn't it?''

Brenna swallowed hard, glancing from her daughter to Colt, then back again. ''Charlie…I don't…know…that riding a horse is something that we should…consider at this…point in time… considering all of the complications that have—''

''That means no,'' Charlie said with a heavy, shoulder-lifting sigh, turning to Colt, looking crestfallen. ''Whenever she starts using those big words and sentences it always means…no.''

''Now, Charlie,'' Brenna began.

''Wait a minute.'' Colt decided he'd better step into the fray, since he had, unwittingly, been the instigator, not to mention the cause of this particular little complication. ''Now, don't go jumping to conclusions, kid.'' Colt stepped forward, speaking to

Charlie, but gauging the worry on Brenna's face correctly. "Your mother hasn't said no—exactly."

"She will." Charlie's chin poked out and she slumped to the bed cross-legged, then rested her elbows on her skinned, bony knees and her crestfallen chin in her hands.

"Let's give her a chance," Colt said carefully, his gaze on Brenna's. He could see the worry and the fear on her face, in her eyes, and realized with a start that maybe she didn't quite trust him with the safety of her child.

He felt a momentary flash of hurt, then realizing how much he didn't know about what the doc and Charlie had been through, not to mention the fact that their initial encounter hadn't exactly boded well for his character, and he could understand her hesitation.

He'd learned one thing about the doc in the past four days: she was passionately protective about the kids, especially Charlie.

So how could he fault her for that?

He couldn't he realize, but it only made him more curious to find out more about her. A woman didn't come by that wariness naturally.

"Doc, listen to me." He made a move to take her hands, then remembering the bandages, let his own hands drop to his sides. "I can assure you all of the Blackwells are excellent horsemen. We've been riding since we could walk."

"Yes, but..." Brenna's voice trailed off. She glanced at him, her eyes pleading. "Charlie's never been on a horse,'' she said carefully. ''And you've been riding since you could...*walk.*'' Her gaze never left his, willing him to understand.

He did. Instantly. She could see it in the look on his face, the way his gaze went to Charlie then back to her. Brenna let out a pent-up sigh of relief.

''Yeah, I know, doc,'' he said quietly, so quietly only she could hear. She merely stared at him in surprised silence.

They'd managed to communicate without using words in a way that seemed way too intimate, and far too personal. Oh, she'd heard, and read that couples who were close, intimate were sometimes were able to communicate with just a look, but she'd never had it happen to her. Not with a man. It stunned her, knocking her off balance again.

Something that was becoming a habit, she realized with dismay.

Colt's gaze, soft, sweet and entirely too understanding snagged hers and Brenna felt a shiver of awareness recklessly race over her, reminding her of this morning. Of his touch. His kiss. The feel of his hard masculine body pressed against hers. The need that had come from nowhere, nearly spiraling out of control.

She had to stop thinking like this, she scolded herself, glancing at her daughter to get some balance and some perspective. She had to stop feeling these things—especially for Colt—they were a clear-cut path to heartache.

''Brenna.'' Her name was a mere whisper on his

lips, causing her to look at him. ''I know that you think their might be...obstacles,'' he said delicately, glancing affectionately at Charlie, who was back to preening at herself in the mirror. ''But I talked to Hunter about it yesterday. He doesn't think there's any reason why Charlie couldn't learn to ride. She's physically strong, has great balance, not to mention incredibly stamina if her checker-cheating ability is any indication,'' he added with that heartbreaking grin. ''And either me, Cutter or Hunter will be with the kids at all times. Even Endy's offered to pitch in,'' he added, mentioning the ranch handyman who had once been a neighbor of his sister Sara's. Endy had accompanied Sara to Texas for their first meeting, and Endy had ended up falling in love with Sadie, and signing on as a handyman at the Blackwell ranch. ''The kids will never be alone. Never be in any danger.'' He laid a hand on Brenna's shoulder.

''Still—'' She chewed her lower lip in worry.

''Brenna,'' he said softly, giving her shoulder a gentle squeeze. ''I would never, ever do anything to jeopardize any of the kids' health or safety.'' His gaze searched hers. ''Do you believe me?''

Mesmerized by his touch, by the soothing gentleness of his voice, by the reassurances in his tone, she couldn't speak, only nod, knowing that with him touching her, looking at her, he could probably make her believe anything.

''Y...es,'' she finally managed to whisper, realizing the impact of what she was saying. She'd never, ever trusted anyone—especially a man—where her daughter's welfare was concerned. Experience had taught her trusting a man blindly, especially with her child's welfare, was a costly mistake, one she could never again afford to make.

"I believe you." Her eyes slid closed and Brenna tried to gather her wits, wondering what on earth was happening to her. And she realized dully, she *did* believe him, did trust him. In spite of the fact that she'd been convinced the man hated children, his every word, his every action had said otherwise.

He had a calming gentleness with her daughter, a camaraderie that only came from someone who was not only comfortable with children, but more importantly *liked* them.

She saw no hint of impatience or anger in him. No sense of imposition or frustration. No sign of annoyance or buried hostility or animosity.

Colt's emotions, feelings and actions toward Charlie seemed truly...genuine.

It was puzzling.

How, she wondered, had she ever thought this man didn't like children?

It made her wonder if there something in his past, something she didn't know about that made him act, or rather react the way he had the first day they met.

Colt Blackwell was turning out to be a complicated puzzle.

Watching and listening to the interplay between the adults in the mirror, Charlie suddenly perked up, a hopeful look on her face. "So does this mean Colt can teach me to ride?'' she asked in excitement, turning to watch her mother carefully. ''Does it, Ma? Does it?''

Aware that both sets of eyes were on her, waiting, Brenna let a heart beat pass, then another. Taking a deep breath, she smiled.

''I guess it does, honey,'' she said cautiously, glancing at Colt, feeling warmed by the look in his eye.

''Yesss!'' Charlie let loose a yell, then leapt up to launch herself into Colt's arms. ''I'm gonna learn to ride.''

Laughing, Colt caught Charlie on the fly as she wrapped arms and legs—braces and all—around him, planting kisses all over his face.

''Thankyou. Thankyou.'' Charlie said. ''A horse. It was my bestest dream.'' Charlie let loose another yell, waving her arms high in the air, as Colt held her, swinging around in a circle. ''Wait till I tell Tommy.'' She rolled her eyes. ''He's gonna die. Just die.''

''Charlie!'' Horrified by her daughter's unabashed actions, and unsure how Colt would react to her daughter's reckless affection, not to mention having her child wrapped around him like sticky wallpaper, Brenna was on her feet immediately.

''Charlie!'' Near panicked, and forgetting about her own injuries, she reached to take Charlie from

Colt's arms, but the look he shot her froze her in her tracks.

"Take it easy, Doc," Colt said gently. "It's not the first time I've held a kid."

"No, I'm sure it's not. It's...just..." Stammering, Brenna chewed her lip, feeling foolish, feeling a rush of buried emotions that came out of nowhere, rocking the fragile security she'd built for herself and her daughter. "It's just that...well..." Her voice trailed off and she merely stared at Colt helplessly.

How could she ever explain? Or put into words the fears, the guilt, the torment she'd lived with so long.

"Hey Doc, you all right?" He was watching her carefully, wondering why her face had drained of color the moment Charlie had leapt in his arms. Something was going on here, something he didn't understand.

He understood her need to protect her child, but this was something more. Something much more.

"Yes..." Brenna said, tossing her hair back. "Of course, I'm...fine."

"Charlie." Gently, Colt set her on her feet, bending down so he was eye level with her. "Why don't you go tell Tommy your news?"

"Can I?" Excitement shone from Charlie's eyes and she could barely contain herself. "Could I tell everybody?"

"Everybody in the world," he confirmed with a grin, ruffling her hair. "But make sure you also tell everybody they're all going to learn how to ride, too."

"Really?" Charlie's eyes went wide as saucers. "Everybody?"

He nodded. "Absolutely everybody." He paused, then frowned. "Except Sadie. Sadie cooks, she doesn't ride." Sadie had made that abundantly clear, loud and clear, the first year she'd joined the Blackwells.

"That's okay," Charlie said, scratching her head. "She cooks real good." Lifting her arms to him in a gesture of pure trust, Colt found his throat constricting.

He picked Charlie up by the armpits, making her giggle again, then planted a loud, smacking kiss to her forehead. "Scoot now, kid. I'll be along in a minute." He gave her behind an affectionate pat, before sending her on her way.

Embarrassed by her behavior at Charlie's unabashed affection toward Colt, yet touched more than she could believe possible by his open acceptance of her daughter, Brenna started to follow her daughter out the door, only to have Colt reach for her wrist, his fingers warm and gentle as a silken manacle, stopping her.

"Not so fast, Doc. I think we should talk."

She swallowed hard, aware that he was touching her again, and she was enjoying it. Again.

"Talk." Brenna licked her dry lips and avoided

his gaze. "Fine." Her chin lifted. "What would you like to talk about?"

"About the fact that you almost tossed your cookies when Charlie leapt into my arms, and I want to know why?" He cocked his head, looking at her curiously. "I thought you said you trusted me with her. Did you think I'd drop her? Hurt her?"

"Of course not," she said with some heat, ashamed that she'd made him think that. "It's not that, Colt. Really."

"Then what is it?"

"It's just...Charlie hasn't been around men very much, and..." She hated the shakiness in her voice, but couldn't help it.

"And?" His fingers tightened on her wrist as if sensing she'd bolt if she could.

"Well, some men wouldn't be...pleased to have a child leaping on them, hugging them, kissing them." Her voice had dropped to a vacant whisper, and Colt looked at her carefully.

"Hey Doc," he said softly, tugging her wrist, drawing her closer. "This is me. Not 'some' man. And any man who didn't relish and treasure a kid's affection—any kid's affection—is an idiot."

Her gaze lifted to his, stunned, hopeful. Scared. "But what about...what about Charlie's..."

"Handicap?" he finished for her. "Look, Doc, if you're worried that it bothers me, you're worrying for nothing. Far as I'm concerned, Charlie's a normal kid." He shrugged. "So she wears glasses and leg braces. So what? Tommy's in a chair, and Eddy the Boss wears glasses thick enough to start ants on fire. So what? None of those things take anything away from how wonderful those kids are. Hell, everyone's got some kind of handicap or disability, even you and I. On some it's just more visible than others, but it's no big deal.'' He shrugged again, tugging her closer, reaching out a hand to once again touch the fading bruise on her cheek. ''Doc, stop worrying, will you?''

She knew she had to say something, to explain her rash behavior. But she needed to swallow the lump in her throat first. Needed to take a deep breath to try to calm the fluttering fear in her heart.

''Charlie's...father...didn't like her...to touch him.''

Colt's gaze narrowed and stared at her hard. ''What?'' His eyes darkened, and a muscle in his jaw clenched. ''What did you just say?''

Brenna sighed, wishing she could just take a step forward, and lean her head on his shoulder, and let him wrap his arms around her so she would feel safe, calm, protected even if just for a little while while she poured out the whole miserable story.

She'd been alone and lonely for so long, and held so much pain inside her heart for so long that now, it was all threatening to come spewing out. But she knew she wouldn't—couldn't. She couldn't ever need or lean on a man ever again. Not just for her sake, but for Charlie's as well. She had no choice but to be strong.

"Her...father..." Brenna swallowed again. "He didn't want Charlie," she whispered, her voice and eyes stricken. "When he found out she would never be...normal, he didn't want her. He wanted to send her away. He was...embarrassed about Charlie's problems. He never paid much attention to her, and rarely touched her. If she touched him, or tried to hug or kiss him, he...cringed and shrunk away from her."

"Damn!" Colt felt as if someone had just kicked him in the chest. Instinctively, Colt tugged her closer to wrap his arms tightly around her. Now he understood why she went pale as the moon when Charlie had leapt into his arms.

She feared he'd have the same reaction as Charlie's father. She thought he'd reject her child.

It hurt, far worse than anything he'd ever imagined. But not nearly as much as it must have hurt the doc and Charlie.

He hoped Charlie's dad was dead simply because it would save him the trouble of killing the man for his actions and behavior.

He didn't understand a man—any man—who didn't want or love his own children, regardless of their physical or mental condition.

"Doc, I'm sorry."

"It's not your—"

"Sorry about what an idiot the guy was. Sorry he

hurt you. Sorrier still he hurt Charlie.'' While he spoke, he ran his hands up and down her back wanting to soothe, to comfort, wanting to take the pain she'd been carrying, and share it.

She was close enough now for him to smell her scent. It was sweet and achingly familiar now, causing a curl of desire to snake through him.

He banked it down, and thought of Charlie, and his eyes slid closed on a wave of unabashed love. The kid was a pistol, how could anyone not love that pint-sized urchin?

Another thought hit him, and with it came understanding.

Now he understood why the doc was so fiercely protective of her kid—of all her kids. She was protecting them from those who might hurt them, intentionally or not. And why shouldn't she? It was understandable. She'd learned the hard way how cruel people could be, including her own husband—Charlie's father.

His respect and admiration for her grew and he shifted his weight, bringing her closer, needing her closer.

Once again the feeling—the need—to protect, to possess nearly overwhelmed him. This time he didn't stop to deny or understand it.

''He was a jackass, Doc,'' he whispered. ''Pure and simply.''

''He wanted to put Charlie away in a home. Someplace where she wouldn't be an embarrassment to him. He thought his money could buy him out of anything unpleasant in life and used it accordingly.''

''And Charlie was just another one of those unpleasant things in his life?'' Shaking his head in disgust, Colt continued to stroke her back. The top of her head came just to his chin, and he could smell her sweet scent once again. It teased his senses, making the ache and need grow.

He couldn't remember when the ache for her, or the need for her had begun, he only knew it was here, strong and vital. It scared the daylights out of him. But not enough to send him running, not now, not with her warm in his arms, and her fears showing on her sleeve.

''Doc, listen to me. If Charlie's father couldn't see or appreciate what a great kid he had, then he didn't deserve her.'' He drew back to look at her. ''Or you,'' he added in a whisper, watching her eyes widen in surprise.

Her lips parted to say something, but no words came out. Their eyes met, held, then clung. Longing swept over him at the purely wounded look in her eyes. There was a fractured innocence about her, a haunting vulnerability that she hid behind that cool, calm facade. She wasn't at all what he thought she was. The more he got to know her, the less he knew her, he realized.

Unlike most women he knew, who'd take advantage of their situation, Brenna had guarded it, and held it tightly to her heart, not asking for or wanting sympathy, wanting only to protect her kid—all the kids.

She'd used her hurt and disappointment to grow strong. Now he understood where her fierce streak of independence came from. It was a form of protection.

Something he understood well.

If she didn't need or lean on anyone, she could never be hurt again.

"Come on now, Doc," he whispered when he heard her sniffle, felt a sob shake her slender body. He held her closer, pressing his lips to her temple. "Don't cry, please? He's not worth your tears."

"I'm not crying for him," she managed to whisper. "But I guess for Charlie." Lifting her head, she managed a smile. "And for me." She sniffled. "I guess I'm just feeling a bit sorry for myself."

"I doubt that," he said. "But if you are, it's understandable. You've been through a hell of a lot." He wasn't just talking about the past week. Having been married to a jerk, no wonder she was so scared and wary around men.

Brenna sniffled, trying to control her tears. It had been a long time since she'd ever discussed this with anyone. Shame had held her a silent prisoner. Now that she'd opened up, she found she couldn't stop.

"For so long I was ashamed, Colt, ashamed that I had married a man who could be so...cold. So cruel to his own child. I should have seen it, known it." She took the hanky Colt pressed into her hand, then wiped her nose. "But I didn't. I was so young—" She shook her head. "That's no excuse," she admitted. "I should have known."

"How the hell could you have known?"

She shook her head, unable to explain the inexplicable obligation all mothers felt toward their children. "There was guilt as well," she added, taking a deep breath. "I had so much guilt about what had happened—"

"What the hell did you have to feel guilty about?" he asked with a frown.

She inhaled slowly, hoping to get the words out. "I blamed myself," she whispered. "Charlie was born prematurely. Her lungs weren't fully developed, so she needed oxygen. It saved her life, but did permanent damage to her vision." She shuddered, remembering that horrifying, frightening time. "I felt guilty because my body couldn't carry her to full-term. I felt as if my body betrayed me, and because of it, my child suffered."

"Oh Doc. It's not your fault. People think a woman gets pregnant and nine months later a kid pops out all pink and perfect, and you know what, if you're very, very fortunate it happens that way, but sometimes, it doesn't, for whatever reason, but no one's to blame." He tilted her chin. "Especially you. You're a wonderful, loving mother, not just to Charlie, but to all those kids." He drew back to look at you. "So what did you do, Doc? When your husband wanted to put Charlie away?"

She met his gaze, his eyes clear, her voice steady. "I left him."

Colt nodded in approval. "It was the least he deserved."

She shrugged. "It's done and over with. Charlie and I survived."

"And thrived," he added with a smile. "Not to mention what you've done for all your other kids."

"I do love them, Colt. All of them as if they were my own." Sniffling, she wiped her eyes.

"And you thought it was necessary to tell me that?" he asked with a laugh. "Doc, love is written all over your face, your eyes, and it's in your every word whenever you look or talk about those kids." He gave her a measured look. "But there's something I'd like to know."

"What?" She glanced up at him. Their eyes met, held, clung, and Brenna shivered, snuggling closer to him, savoring his warmth, the comfort of his arms, knowing she couldn't allow herself to want or enjoy it for it was too risky.

But she'd give herself this moment. This rare moment of indulgence. Surely she could allow herself just one moment?

He stroked a finger down her cheek, gently touched the fading bruise. "You protect all the kids, Doc. But who protects you?"

"W-what?" It wasn't at all what she'd expected him to ask.

"You take care of all the kids, and protect them

as well.'' He slid his hand to cup her cheek, brushing a tear away with his thumb. ''But who protects and takes care of you?''

''N-no one,'' she finally stammered. She lifted her chin. ''I don't need anyone to protect or take care of me.'' She'd worked hard to take care of herself, to not need anyone, ever, especially a man. And she was certain she'd succeeded.

Until she met Colt.

Now, she wasn't quite so sure. And it frightened her. As did he.

One dark eyebrow rose in question. ''That's where you're wrong, Doc,'' he said quietly.

She was so close. Too close. It was arousing all kinds of feelings, emotions. The kind that usually made him itchy and nervous. He knew he had to walk away from her, and stay away from her. It was the only way to preserve his sanity. She was edging in too close to him emotionally. Not trusting himself when she was so close, he bent and brushed his lips against her forehead, down her cheek to nuzzle her mouth.

She moaned softly, and the sound tore threw him. He let his mouth take hers in a fiercely possessive kiss that left them both staggered and breathless.

Shaken, Colt stepped back, letting his arms drop to his side. If he didn't walk away now, he feared he might not be able to.

''You know, Doc, maybe it's about time someone

showed you that you *do* need someone to protect—and take care of you."

Before she could open her mouth, he turned, and walked out of the room, leaving her standing there, fists clenched, heart pounding, staring after him.

Chapter Six

It was seriously dark and very late by the time Colt let himself in the back door of the sprawling Blackwell Ranch. He'd stayed on at the construction site of the Home later than usual just to be certain everyone would be gone by the time he got home.

Something he'd been doing for more than a week now in an effort to keep his distance from the doc.

The moment the kitchen door shut behind him, he smelled it, and groaned. There was no disguising that smell. He should have known. Sadie and her traditions.

Christmas trees.

The whole house reeked of pine. On the Friday, two weeks before Christmas, Sadie started her annual tradition of preparing the house for the holiday.

Grateful now that he'd stayed at the site late, Colt walked into the kitchen, flipped on a light, and pulled a beer out of the fridge, deliberately avoiding looking at the large decorated tree sitting in the corner of the big family kitchen and the twinkling lights that cast a soft amber glow throughout the room.

"Did you have any dinner?" Sadie asked with a scowl, marching into the kitchen to snatch the bottle of beer out of his hand just as he tipped the bottle back to take a drink. "No drinking until you've eaten. You know my rules."

Although Sadie's age was a closely guarded secret, she still looked to him the same as she had the day he'd arrived on the Blackwells' doorsteps.

Short and stout as a fireplug, with steel gray hair pulled back neatly into a bun, and snappy blue eyes that could freeze you on the spot, Sadie never seemed to change. She always wore a print housedress covered by a crisp, freshly pressed and starched apron, and always smelled like vanilla.

Colt looked longingly at the beer. "Come on, Sadie," he wheedled, reaching for the beer, only to have her slap his hand away. "I just left the Home, and I didn't have time to eat. I put in almost twenty hours today. One beer on an empty stomach isn't going to kill me."

She paused and took a long, slow look at him. "You look like hell, boy. I didn't raise you to be a fool, working yourself night and day, not eating. What is the matter with you?" Planting her hands on her ample hips, she narrowed her gaze on him. "And why aren't you out partying with your brothers? You guys aren't fighting again, are you?" She shook her head. "'Cuz if you are, big as you are, I'll take a switch to you, I will."

Grinning, he shook his head. It was an idle threat Sadie had been making for as long as he could remember.

"Course not, although I was tempted to deck Cutter this afternoon, but I managed to restrain myself."

"Humph." Cocking her head, she gave him a measured look. "So why aren't you out with 'em? Not like you to pass up a good time. You ailing, boy?" She took a step forward, stood on tiptoe and placed a hand to his forehead, checking for fever the way she had when he was a boy.

Colt resisted the temptation to laugh, and willingly let Sadie mother him. Even though they were all grown, Sadie still treated him and his brothers as if they were wayward five-year-olds with about as much sense.

And all three would admit they wouldn't have it any other way.

He grabbed her hand and kissed it. "Nah, I'm fine, Sadie. Right as rain as a matter of fact. I just missed you." He bent down and planted a loud kiss on her rouged cheek.

"Go on with you now," she said with a blush, touching her cheek where he'd kissed her. "Go use that charm on someone it'll do some good."

He glanced around. It was far too quiet in the house. "Where's the kids?"

Sadie's face lit up. "They're all asleep, including Endy." She beamed at the mention of her husband, even after a year. "Those young'uns are something else. Ran me and Endy ragged today. But we loved it." She laughed, her face shining with love. "That man is so good with them babies, I tell you, it's a shame he didn't have any of his own."

"He's got you, Sadie." Colt draped an arm around her shoulder. "And us, now."

"Yeah." Sadie looked at him, then shook her head. "Lordy, I'm sure gonna miss those babies when they're gone," she said wistfully.

Only Sadie would think dropping six kids on her at one time, with no notice, a few weeks before a major holiday was fun. No wonder they all loved her so much.

"Yeah, well, remember that when Sara gives birth to twins and you've got kids squalling all night long."

Sadie grinned. "I can't wait. It's about time you boys started having babies of your own. I miss having someone to spoil."

"Ah come on, now, Sadie, you can still spoil me."

She gave him a friendly whack on the arm. "I've always spoiled you," she said with a grin. "And you know it."

"That I do." Grinning, he dragged her closer to plant another kiss on her cheek. "Have I told you how much I love you, lately?"

Embarrassed, she sniffed the air, then scowled. "I love you, too, boy, but you need a shower. You smell like a polecat." She gave him a quick hug, wrapping her chubby arms around his waist, like he used to do to her when he was too small to reach her. "Now, go have yourself a shower, and I'll rustle you up some grub," she said, handing him back his beer. "And don't tell your brothers I let you have a beer without eating," she added with a scowl.

Laughing, Colt kissed her again. "I won't."

By the time he'd showered and eaten, the overwhelming scent of the pine Christmas trees, coupled with the decorations all over the house were driving Colt crazy. He'd managed to keep his feelings, his memories in check so far this year, but he figured the kids, and all the work he had to do helped. It gave him little time to think.

Except about Brenna.

After checking on the kids, and assuring himself they were all well and sound asleep, he grabbed another beer, then headed out onto the porch.

He'd just stepped through the doorway, when he heard the old-fashioned porch swing creak. Letting the screen door shut quietly behind him, Colt stood transfixed.

Brenna was sitting on the swing, gently swaying back and forth. Dressed in faded jeans, and a soft sweater that caressed her curves, she looked small and vulnerable. The soft yellow light from the porch cast soft shadows over the planes and angles of her face.

He was absolutely certain he had never seen anything so beautiful. Something clutched his heart, moving it, nearly taking his breath away.

"Why aren't you out with Cutter and Hunter?" he asked softly, drinking in the sight of her.

"Oh!" Brenna's hand went to her heart and she jumped at the sound of his voice. Turning toward him, she flashed him a shaky smile. "Colt. I didn't realize you were home." Nervous, she glanced down at her laced fingers, then lifted one hand to push a tumble of curls off her cheek. "If you'd like some privacy, I'll be happy to go inside. It's getting late anyway."

She stood, and started to move past him, but he reached out an arm and laced it around the front of her waist, drawing her close, stopping her.

"No, actually what I'd like is some company," he said quietly. She was pressed against him, side to side, close enough for him to be intoxicated by her sweet scent, to feel the soft curve of her hip pressed against his.

It had been over a week since he'd laid eyes on her, touched her and now, he felt as if it had been years. The edginess that had been crawling along his spine, the uneasiness, the feeling that something was wrong or missing seemed to evaporate at the sight and touch of her.

"Are you sure?" she asked hesitantly and he grinned in return.

"Positive." Taking her hand, he brought her with him back toward the swing, watching as she sat, curling her long, jean-clad legs beneath her.

He sat down next to her, not trusting himself to get too close.

"So how come you didn't go over to Bailey's for her annual Christmas party with the rest of the family?" Tilting his beer back to take a sip, he watched her.

"I'm not much in the party spirit," she admitted, glancing out into the darkness.

"How are your hands?" he asked with a frown, picking one up, and turning it over to examine her palm. "Hunter said he took the bandages off yesterday." With another small frown, he lifted her other hand and gave it the same careful examination.

"They're fine." She shrugged. "A few minor scars, and a little pinker and softer than normal, but Hunter said that's normal, considering."

He lifted one hand to his mouth, pressing a whisper of a kiss against the tender palm. "I'm glad." He continued kissing her hand, gently, around and up her wrist, savoring the taste and scent of her. Her scent was stronger here, at her pulse point. He inhaled deeply, savoring and holding the scent in his lungs. He was certain he couldn't get enough of her. "Your pulse is scrambling," he said, pleased.

She snatched her hand free, embarrassed by her reaction and annoyed by his ego.

"My...my hands are still a bit...tender." It was a lie, but she was far too proud to admit her heart was fluttering like a trapped butterfly. Her skin tingled from his touch, his kiss and a shiver was racing along her spine, making her acutely aware of him.

"So how come you're not out partying with your brothers?" she asked, anxious to change the subject. Deliberately, she kept her voice cool although her insides were shaking.

She hadn't seen him in a week, and knew he'd been avoiding her. One part of her was grateful, simply because she didn't know how to handle him, or what happened to *her* when he was near.

Another part was annoyed simply because in such a short period of time he had become such a vital part of her life, because he'd insisted upon it, insisted upon having her and the kids move in, really leaving her no choice but to see him, get to know him, and now, he was avoiding her.

It hurt, she realized.

And she simply didn't know what to do about it.

There was nothing to do, she realized. Why should it matter if he deliberately avoided her? There could be nothing between them regardless of how he made her feel or what he made her feel.

She'd seen two sides of him, two different sides, and she wasn't certain which was the real Colt. The man she'd seen the day they'd met at the Children's Home; a man who could be cold and careless about children as well as Christmas. Or the completely compassionate, caring man she'd seen in the days since.

Which was the real Colt?

She realized she wasn't sure and it made her naturally cautious.

"I'm not much in the mood for partying, either."

He took another sip of his beer. "And I don't much like Christmas," he admitted with a sigh, making her turn toward him.

Something about the tone of his voice had her heart fluttering in anxiety.

"I gathered that." She watched him carefully. There was something in his eyes, in his voice that had aroused her curiosity. "Any particular reason?" she asked, deliberately keeping her voice light.

She didn't want to pry, but she was desperately curious to know why he was so ornery about Christmas. It was so odd. For a man who was so close to his family, not liking a holiday that was the embodiment of family was confusing.

Silence hung in the air for a long moment. The only sound was the creaking of the porch swing, and the hoot of a lonely owl in the distance.

"I had...a little brother," Colt began quietly, not looking at her, but staring straight ahead into the darkness. "His name was Cade." He paused, swallowed, then took another sip of his beer because his throat had gone dry. "He died around Christmas. I haven't been real fond of the holiday since." Colt tipped his head back, then blew out a weary breath.

He'd never spoken a word about this with anyone, but for some reason now, he wanted to tell Brenna, wanted to explain—that his hating Christmas had nothing to do with her or her kids.

But he simply couldn't. He knew emotionally he wasn't ready to tell her the whole story. Maybe he'd never be ready. And with the time of year, and with his emotions already in turmoil over her, he knew he was treading on dangerous ground.

Best to retreat, he thought wisely.

"Oh Colt." Her hand went to his arm, to comfort, to soothe. "I'm so sorry. I had no idea. It must have been awful for you, losing your brother." Now, she understood a little bit about his not liking Christmas, particularly if his brother had died around the holiday, but his reaction still seemed way out of proportion.

She had a feeling there was a great deal more to this story than Colt was letting on, but from his reaction, she knew this wasn't the time to ask.

"It was a long time ago," he said gruffly, his tone of voice making it clear the subject was off-limits. "And not something I care to discuss."

His words, his body language stung. Rejection wasn't anything new, she'd dealt with it for years from her husband, but she'd forgotten how miserable it made her feel.

Bristling at his response, Brenna withdrew emotionally and physically. She removed her hand from his arm, feeling embarrassed and hurt by his reaction.

"I'm sorry," she said again, more stiffly, not certain what else to say.

"Not a problem." His voice was clipped, his tone short. "Let's just drop it, shall we?" Rubbing a weary hand over his face, Colt sighed again.

Leaning back in the swing, he touched his toe to the porch floor and allowed the swaying of the swing to soothe him. He let his eyes slide closed, and tried to block the memories from his mind.

But they still kept coming, making his mood even more foul.

For long moments they sat in silence, the only sound the gentle creek of the porch swing. Finally, Brenna broke the silence.

"Can I ask you a question?"

The tone of her voice had him looking up and at her curiously. "Of course. Shoot." Her slow smile made him realize what he'd said. He held up his hand. "I'm the sheriff, but don't take that literally."

She cocked her head to study him. "Have I done something to offend you?"

He let the question hang in the air, taking a sip of his beer in order to stall. Lord, he just was not in the mood for this.

"No," he finally said, turning to look at her. "Why do you ask?"

"Because you've deliberately been avoiding me the past week."

"Nope," he said, trying out a grin and hoping to charm his way out of this. He didn't know how to deal with what he was feeling for her, what she made him feel. "Just been busy."

His answer, so clearly a lie, infuriated her. She jumped to her feet as her emotions tangled in a rush of anger and hurt. "You could at least have the courtesy of being honest with me, Sheriff."

She glared down at him, pushing her hair off her face when a faint breeze stirred it. "You're the one who invited—no, insisted we come and stay with you. If you're tired of us, or if I've done something to offend you, the least you could do is be honest."

Taking a deep breath, Colt rose slowly, setting his beer on the ledge of the window sill. His movements were so slow, so deliberate, they had her taking a step backward.

"Are you saying I haven't been busy?" Shame battled with his ego. He wasn't a man who liked to admit he was afraid—of anything, especially a woman. But that was the truth of it, the reason he was avoiding her. But damned if he was going to admit it. Or explain it.

Especially to her.

"I'm saying you're lying about avoiding me," she stammered, wondering why she felt like weeping. Perhaps because he'd so easily lied to her. Coming right on the heels of what she felt was a rejection only made it hurt more.

Something else her husband had been so good at. Lies and rejection. For her. For Charlie. Old wounds that had never fully healed, opened, festered.

"You don't believe I've been busy?" Colt asked again, knowing he was itching for a fight. Something—anything—to clear his thoughts and cleanse his emotions. With her so close, she was playing havoc with his self-control. He knew he should stay away from her, but knew he simply couldn't. And it only added to his annoyance with himself, with her.

Brenna lifted her chin. "You may have been

busy, but you've also been avoiding me and I don't understand why, or why you won't admit it. A little truth goes a long way, Sheriff.'' She gave her head a toss. ''You should try it sometime.''

''That does it.'' He grabbed her hand, hanging on when she started to protest. ''Let's go,'' he said, tugging her hand to get her going as he started moving across the porch.

''I'm not going—'' She dug her heels in, refusing to be tugged along like a misbehaved household pet.

''Yes, you are,'' he said, coming to a halt and rounding on her until they were standing toe to toe.

She was back to being cool, calm and classy. He could see it in her stance, her eyes, the cool, calm way she gave that gorgeous head a toss.

But the image didn't fit anymore, not now that he'd gotten to know her. It was an image he'd begun to realize was nothing more than a facade to cover her fears, her vulnerabilities. She wore it like a cloak, a form of protection, and if you didn't look deeper, beyond it, it was all you saw. But he saw so much more.

He tugged her down the step, his voice clipped. ''I want to show you *exactly* what's been keeping me busy the past week.''

Chapter Seven

"Oh Colt. I can't believe it," Brenna breathed, stunned. I just can't believe it." With her hands pressed to her mouth, Brenna climbed out of the car, staring through the veils of darkness toward the Home.

Although the night was pitch-black, the street-lights cast enough of a glow for her to see the enormous amount of work that had been done since the night of the fire. Moved beyond belief, she turned to him, her eyes welling with tears.

"How—when—" She shook her head, unable to believe her eyes.

She was embarrassed by her treatment of him, by her accusations when now, she could see he truly had been busy. Doing something for her, for the children. Guilt washed over her like a heavy mist, making her feel ashamed and miserable.

"When did you do all of this?" Her eyes scanned the building from roof to ground, taking everything in. It didn't even resemble the same place. "*How* did you do all of this?"

"Well, I didn't do it all myself," he said with a laugh, coming around the car to take her hand as they started walking closer to the building. "Be careful, there's still a lot of work to be done, and even though the guys cleaned up as best as can every night, this is still basically a construction site, and dangerous." He tightened his hold on her hand. "Step lively," he cautioned, helping her over a pile of boards.

Still staring at the building, Brenna shook her head as she tugged him forward, anxious to see everything. "I just...I can't believe it." Overcome, she turned to him, her eyes swimming again. "I don't remember much from the night of the fire, but I remember enough to know how extensive the damage was. I don't understand how you've managed to—"

"Two crews of men working two shifts of nine hours each day, every day since the fire."

"Crews?" Frowning, she clutched his hand tightly, needing to hold onto him right now, needing to touch him. "Where did you get the crews from?"

He laughed. "Once everyone in town found out about the fire, just about every able-bodied man volunteered their time. Cutter drove into Dallas the day after the fire and ordered all the materials. By the time they were delivered, we had the crews assembled, and work divided." He laughed. "Blackwell may be a small town, but we've got a lot of talented tradesmen, not to mention that fact that my brothers and I all worked our way through college doing construction jobs." Shaking his head, he laughed again. "My dad always said the experience would come in handy some day."

Surprised, she stopped and turned, merely staring at him. "You worked your way through college?"

"I had a feeling that would surprise you," he said with a grin, pausing beside a stacked pile of lumber, and indicating she should sit.

"I...I..." Her voice trailed off and she glanced up at him helplessly. "It does," she admitted softly.

"Because I'm a Blackwell?" He tilted her chin up so she was forced to look at him. There was something in his eyes, something she couldn't identify, she only knew that it made her blood heat, and her heart tumble. "Let me tell you something, Brenna. My father may be the largest and wealthiest rancher in these parts, but he's a firm believer in working for your keep." Settling one booted foot on the pile of lumber next to her, he nodded toward the Home. "Ever wonder why my parents have such a powerful interest in the Home?"

"I thought it was just because they're very civic-minded and care about their community."

"They are that," he admitted. "But it's a whole lot more. My father grew up in the Children's Home," he said softly, and something in his voice had her heart turning over, and her head turning toward him.

"You're father, Justin Blackwell grew up *here.*" She glanced over her shoulder at the Home, then back at Colt, trying to put all the puzzle pieces that comprised Colt Blackwell into their proper place.

But they weren't fitting.

Too many pieces were still missing, she realized.

"Yeah," he admitted, blowing out a deep breath. "You see, my dad was orphaned and dumped at the Home when he was just a kid. He didn't have anything, not even a name." He glanced down at her. "Ever wonder why our last name is the same as the town?" He didn't give her a chance to answer. "Because my dad never knew his real name. So when he was eighteen, he lit out of the Home vowing to make something of himself. He didn't have anything, not even a name, so he took the name of the town so he'd have something to call his own. He met my mother, and the rest is history."

The love in his eyes, in his voice for his father was so evident, it had her getting to her feet. A man who loved so deeply, so openly couldn't be the unfeeling, cold man she thought him to be.

"Oh Colt." She lifted a hand to his cheek, surprised and moved by what he'd told her. She had been wrong about him, had misjudged him. "I didn't know. I had no idea."

"And here all this time you thought I was just some spoiled rich kid, using my family's money to make life easier for me, right?"

"I'm sorry, Colt," she said softly, suffused with guilt. She'd hurt him, she realized, with her inaccurate assumptions and unfair accusations. It hurt her to know she'd hurt him.

"Brenna," he said, covering her hand with his. "We both obviously had a lot of misconceptions about the other." Easily, he slid his other arm around her waist, drawing her close. The night's darkness seemed to wrap around them in a cocoon of intimacy.

In the distance, an owl hooted, and the wind swayed gently. Neither noticed.

She took a step closer, until she was pressed against him. Heart to heart.

"I thought you hated children," she admitted softly.

"Hate kids?" he repeated in alarm. He shook his head, drawer her even closer. "How on earth did you ever come to that conclusion?"

Her gaze searched his as hope flared bright and new in her heart. Because of his late brother perhaps she understand his behavior now. It didn't explain everything, of course, but it was a start.

"That first day, when we spoke on the phone, you were just so rude, and then later when you came to the Home, you were so cold, so callous about...playing Santa, about the kids, tossing your money around, I just figured you hated kids and thought you could use your money to buy you out of anything you found...unpleasant."

He would have laughed at the absurdity, but now

that he knew about her ex-husband, he could see how she would jump to that conclusion. It shamed him that he could have behaved in a manner that in any way resembled her ex.

"I can see how you might have gotten that impression," he admitted. "Nothing could be further from the truth." He glanced into the darkness for a moment, searching for the right words. Words that had always come easily with other women, but then, he was careful to keep things light, charming. With the doc, he wasn't interested in being charming. He merely wanted to assure her, to make her see that he wasn't anything like the man she'd been married to.

He shifted his gaze back to hers. Even in the darkness he could make out her every feature. "Do you know why I've been on everyone's case, making sure they bust their butts, trying to finish this up as quickly as possible?"

"Because you're a great guy?" she said with a saucy smile, trying to use humor to hide the fact that her knees were knocking at his closeness.

His clean, fresh scent was playing havoc with her senses. Need rose up to taunt her, the same need she'd felt whenever he was near. Need that she'd never felt, or even been aware of before. Not with anyone, but him.

Now it was like a starving beast with the scent of food in the air. Her stomach knotted, her heart pounded, and she felt that strange, wonderful tightness begin in her belly as hunger, need for him rose up to mock her.

"So you've finally noticed," he said with a laugh. "But that's not the only reason."

"All right. So tell me why?"

He looked a her for a long moment, a look that had her heart tumbling. "Because Charlie told me she was afraid Santa wouldn't be able to find them if they weren't home." Looking sheepish, he grinned. "I promised her I'd have her home by Christmas."

Moved beyond belief, her mouth opened, but no words came out. Her eyes filled, then spilled over. "Oh, Colt."

"Good Lord," he said in a panic, cupping her cheek and wiping a tear away. "Don't cry. *Please* don't cry."

"I'm not," she insisted, swiping at her nose. "It's just...just...no one has ever cared so much, or done so much for my daughter—for any of the children." Sniffling, she gave him a shaky smile, but her tears still fell. "You know what they call themselves? Brenna's children." A sob broke loose. "Because they don't think anyone else wants or cares about them."

"Oh Brenna." His eyes slid closed and he thought about what she'd told him about Charlie's father. About how he hadn't wanted his daughter; couldn't accept her or her handicap. It made his blood boil. He knew from experience all about parents not wanting kids, about dumping them on doorsteps, or simply abandoning them, or leaving them to fend for themselves.

Yeah, he knew all about those kinds of parents. Because he'd been born with one.

But he realized, Brenna wasn't one of those parents. More importantly, she wasn't like any of the women he'd ever known, and never trusted.

He feared that she was everything he never thought a woman could be. Honest. Caring. Loving. Giving. And so compassionate about the kids—especially the kids in her life—that she made it her life's work.

Unlike his cool, calm birth mother, a woman so cold and callous she'd abandoned her helpless children and allowed one to die a cruel, brutal death, and left the other alone in the world to fend for himself, to mourn and grieve for the rest of his life.

Fortunately, he'd found the love of a good family, a man and a woman who had only love and kindness in their heart, and a capacity for giving that knew no bounds.

Like Brenna, he thought. In some ways, she was just like his adopted mother Emma. She, too, had taken in children no one else had wanted. Taken them in and made them her own, giving them her time, her love, and a home as well as a sense of family and belonging.

At one time he believed there was not another woman alive like Emma Blackwell.

Now, he knew better, knew too, how badly he'd misjudged Brenna.

Drawing her closer, he pressed her head against his shoulder, hoping to still her tears. "I care about your kids—all of them," he specified. "Each and every one of them, braces, glasses, checker-cheating and all. We all do. I can't tell you how much they've added to our lives. To my life." Gently, he ran a comforting hand down the silk of her hair.

With a sigh, Brenna allowed herself to relax against him, giving herself as she once wished and hoped for a moment to just lean on him. To need him without worrying about the consequences. She needed him at this moment, needed his warmth, his comfort, needed to feel his arms around her, holding her, comforting her.

Until she'd met him, she never realized how much she needed this. Perhaps because she'd never needed until him.

Until Colt.

Sniffling, she ordered her body to relax, wrapping her arms around his neck, snuggling closer.

"I was so very wrong about you, Colt." All the feelings that she'd buried inside, all the feelings she'd been denying all these weeks since they'd met, now bubbled to the surface, refusing to be denied any longer.

Her words caused guilt to slide over him like a cold blanket, forcing him to face reality.

"Brenna," he said hesitantly, drawing back to look at her. "Before you anoint me for sainthood, there's something you should know."

Lifting her head, she looked at him, brushing a hand against her eyes to dry her tears. "What?"

"I lied to you tonight."

She sighed heavily. "I know, Colt," she said, pushing her hair off her face.

"You know?" he asked in surprise.

She nodded. "You lied about avoiding me, right?"

"Yeah," he admitted with a sigh. "I...I...I'm not real proud about lying, I'm not usually dishonest."

Her gaze searched his, needing to understand. "Then why did you lie to me?"

He hadn't realized how important this was to her until this moment. It wasn't what he'd lied about, but the fact that he lied at all that was troubling her. He knew her well enough now to read the shadows of doubt, of fear in her eyes.

And he cursed himself.

He'd been doing his damnest to get her to trust him, to show her he wasn't at all like her former husband, but then, he let pride and ego rule his common sense.

Letting his eyes slide closed, Colt realized he had to tell her the truth. Had to tell her why he'd been avoiding her. He knew he'd never felt this way about a woman before, never felt this *need,* oh, there'd been desire, plenty of times, but that was all it was because that was all he'd ever allowed.

But with Brenna, there was need, the need for her was as strong and deep as the need to breathe. He'd been miserable this past week, not seeing her, not touching her, trying to talk himself out of what he was feeling. No words could erase what was in his heart. Not now. And he feared, not ever.

He took a slow, deep breath, allowing the impact of his thoughts to still and settle. She was so close, her scent was infiltrating his lungs with every breath, teasing, taunting, seducing. He had to swallow, tightening his fingers on the curve of her waist to hold her in place.

"I lied to you, Brenna, because I didn't want you to know how much you scare me."

"Scare you?" she repeated in confusion. "How on earth could I possible scare you?"

They were barely a whisper apart. He wasn't certain his mind or his mouth could continue to function with her so close. He had to swallow again.

"You...scare me because of what I feel—because of how and what you make me feel—I've never felt—"

"Shhh." Brenna lifted her fingers to his lips. "Don't. It's all right. I understand," she whispered. "You scare me as well." Her gaze, soft with love, with emotion found his. "I've tried very hard to keep my feelings, my emotions under control, but I don't think I've succeeded very well, at least not where you're concerned."

She never thought she'd ever feel these things for a man, much less admit them. She glanced away, embarrassed now, but knowing that she couldn't deny what was in her heart.

She lifted her chin, and let her gaze find his. "I've

never felt this way about any other man. Not ever, Colt. I've never wanted to feel this way about a man.'' She shivered at the truth of her words, knowing how vulnerable it made her, knowing how easily she could be hurt.

But along with the feelings she had for him came something else: trust.

She couldn't feel this way about a man she didn't trust. She knew that. And in spite of her initial perceptions about him, she'd come to learn that he was a man worth, and worthy of her trust.

Hers and the childrens.

His every word, his every action had proved it these past few weeks. If not in the way he'd treated her, then the way he treated the kids—all of them—had sealed it.

No man could do what he'd done for the kids if he didn't have a kind heart and a loving nature.

Although she had a feeling he wouldn't be going around spouting either or adding them to his resume.

''Brenna.'' He brushed his lips against her forehead, drawing her closer.

''You've given me so much—you've given the children so much,'' she whispered, pressing her head against his shoulder, savoring the strength, the safety she found there. It was something she'd never thought she'd feel, certainly not with a man. ''I don't know what to say...how to thank you.''

He drew back to look at her, his eyes dark. ''So is this gratitude then?'' Disappointment coupled with male pride made his voice sharp. "Because if it is, I don't want—"

With a smile, she laid a hand to his chest, stood on tiptoe, then brushed her lips against his in a whisper of a kiss. "Gratitude is not exactly the word I'd use to describe what I feel for you."

"Brenna." He dragged her closer, pressing his lips to hers in a drugging, possessive kiss that left them both breathless.

"I...I don't know how to handle this." Breathless, Brenna dragged a shaky hand through her hair. "I don't know how to handle these feelings..." She lifted her suddenly shy gaze to his. "I don't know how to handle you."

Still holding her, he let out a frustrated sigh. "It doesn't help much knowing that, Brenna. It only makes it worse on me. I'm trying to be good, here, trying to be a gentlemen. You're not making it any easier."

She smiled in the darkness, pleased that she was having the same effect on him as he was having on her.

She loped her arms around his neck, planting a string of kisses from his chin to his cheek. "You wouldn't want me to lie, would you?" she murmured.

"Yes—no!"

"Yes? No?" She grinned, enjoying herself, and his discomfort. This was a side of him she hadn't seen. Cool, cocky Colt Blackwell was duly and truly flustered.

By her.

For the first time in years, Brenna's female ego soared, and she realized it was a heady feeling.

"Are you flustered, Colt?" she asked with a laugh as she continued to plant soft little kisses over his face, edging closer and closer to his mouth, touching the corner, then darting away in a teasing gesture that had him leaning closer toward her, pulling her more tightly against him.

"Flustered." Colt had to swallow. She was quite aware that she definitely driving him crazy. And if he wasn't mistaken, enjoying every minute of it. But there was no guile, it was purely the pleasure of female discovery.

"Yes," she murmured, finding a particularly sensitive spot right below his left ear that she had an urge to nuzzle. "Flustered." She let her lips slide down the corded column of his tanned neck, making him groan. "Yes, I believe you are." She chuckled, clearly enjoying herself. "Imagine that. Colt Blackwell flustered by a mere woman."

"You talk too much," he said, a moment before he hauled her off her feet, ran his fingers through her hair to tilt her head back, then took her mouth.

His mouth was neither gentle, nor filled with finesse, it merely...possessed.

Hot, punishing, possessive, filled with passion, desire, and more importantly, with love.

She could taste it in his lips, in the way his hands gentled at her waist, the way he cradled her body against his.

Love.

She was absolutely certain she'd never felt it, certainly not like this, not ever before.

It filled her heart and her mind, and comforted her soul. She kissed him back with all the love, the passion she had inside of her.

Other than her husband—since her husband, there had never been anyone else. She never thought she needed it, wanted it, never thought she was destined to feel these powerful female feelings that swamped her now, and made the world spin, and stars swim behind her eyes.

She'd resigned herself to a life alone, thought it better that way, safer; now she knew better. Life wasn't meant to be safe; it was meant to be savored.

Brenna moaned softly as Colt's hands slid from her waist, to caress her back, the motion crushing her swollen breasts against his broad, hard chest.

She moaned again as his tongue darted, teased, then thoroughly seduced her mouth until she was clinging to him.

She was so small, so delicate, Colt thought, gentling his hands, fearing he would hurt her by the strength of his desire, his passion.

He was not a man who lost control often, and never with a woman. But with Brenna he seemed not to have any control left.

All he felt was wants, needs, desires. His body responded, coinciding with his heart, marching in step like a lost, but familiar tune.

God, he wanted her, wanted to ease the ache of

desire that burned through him, sending his heart pounding within his chest, making his knees shake and his body ache.

She wasn't close enough, not nearly close enough. She couldn't seem to get close enough to him. There was barely a breath of air between them, but it still wasn't enough. He let his hands roam the length of her slender back, down to her waist, pausing to gently cup her buttocks, groaning softly as her softness pressed against his hardness.

He was losing control, and he knew he couldn't. Not now. Not like this. Not with her.

He knew she had no experience, knew that this was all knew to her. He could read it in the wonder of her eyes when he kissed her, see it in the flush of her cheeks when he'd kissed her silly.

Reluctantly, and with great effort, he dragged his mouth from hers, his breathing ragging, his body aching.

"Brenna." He said nothing more than her name. Holding her close, heartbeat to heartbeat, he tried to regain control.

Tilting her head back, her gaze, dazed with passion met his.

"Colt."

"No, no words, not now." He wasn't certain he was ready yet to put into words what was in his heart. He pressed his mouth to hers again until she was whimpering softly, her arms wrapping around him to hold him close as he drew back again, knowing he and his heart were fighting a losing battle.

Just one last kiss, he told himself, as he pulled her back to him, not yet fully accepting or understanding that just one more kiss would never be enough.

Chapter Eight

From the age of eight, Colt had never been a sound or easy sleeper. So it wasn't unusual for him to be up at the crack of dawn, long before the rest of the house.

On this last Saturday morning, six short days before Christmas, the sun was just awakening when he stepped out of his adjoining bath where'd he'd indulged himself in a long, cold shower, something he'd been doing a lot of since the night he'd taken Brenna to see the Home. The woman was driving him crazy, and he didn't have a clue what to do about it. More importantly, he'd stopped wondering and worrying what to do about it, which should have worried him more.

It didn't.

This morning, after stepping out of the shower,

he'd just lathered his face with shaving cream when he heard the catch on his bedroom door click.

He froze, swiped his face clean with a towel, then grabbed a robe and tossed it on, wondering what the heck was going on.

"What if he gets mad 'cuz we woke him up?" came a faint frightened whisper he now recognized as Sunshine Mary, a five-year-old with a mop of golden hair who never stopped smiling in spite of the fact that she worried more than the doc. A kid that age shouldn't have any worries, he'd thought more than once.

"Shhh," came Charlie's authoritative reply. "If we're quiet we won't wake him up."

"That's stupid, Charlie," Eddy the Boss hissed. The oldest at seven, Eddy had an IQ somewhere hovering around the brilliant range, and a vocabulary to match. Thus, he was the self-appointed expert on all matters, hence his nickname. "How we gonna ask him if we don't wake him up?" Scowling in pure male superiority, Eddy pushed his oversized glasses up his nose and glared owlishly at Charlie.

Colt froze, waiting. He could hear them clamoring into the room. Leg braces scraping, wheels squeaking. A sneak attack it wasn't.

Deliberately banking a smile, he stood quietly behind the door, waiting to see just what the little munchkins were up to. No good, no doubt, he thought with a grin.

"I gotta go to the bathroom," Tommy whined, making Colt grin. At four, Tommy the tow-headed toddler who had a shiner the night he'd rescued him from the fire, always had to go to the bathroom.

"Hold it," Eddy ordered, as he glanced around, pushing his glasses up his nose once again. "Where's Mikey? And Petey?"

"They went to find Mr. Bubkus. He's loose again," Tommy volunteered, making the group groan in unison.

"Mr. Bubkus?" Eddy was back to scowling behind his glasses.

"But fwogs can't help us," Mary Sunshine whined. "Only Colt could help." Her eyes widened. "But he's not here." The disappointment in Mary Sunshine's voice was so evident, he could cut it with a knife.

"No," Colt said, stepping into the room and shutting his bedroom door behind the mismatched troop. "I'm here."

Mary and Tommy both screeched in alarm, nearly scaring Colt out of his robe. "Easy, easy." He held his hands up in the air, certain his heart would settle in a moment.

"You're supposed to be sleeping," Charlie accused, chin tilted in a way that reminded him of her mother.

"So are you," he pointed out reasonably, crossing his arms across his chest. He cocked his head and looked at the assembled troop. "So why aren't you?"

Four pair of eyes exchanged guilty stares.

Bravely, Eddy moved to the head, meeting Colt's gaze. "We've got to ask you something, sir."

Obviously Eddy had appointed himself the leader of this band, and wanted to talk man to man. "All right," Colt said with a nod of his head.

"But Brenna said we wasn't thupposed to bother you." Mary Sunshine was worrying her lower lip. Instinctively, Colt swung her up in his arms.

"You're not bothering me, Sunshine," he said with a grin. "Now, what do you want to ask me?"

"Cookies," she blurted out nervously, wrapping her arms around his neck. He nodded his head, looking at the remaining trio curiously.

"Cookies. Okay, I get it. You want cookies for breakfast and Baby ate them all?"

"No," echoed the giggling chorus.

"Baby's a dog," Eddy pointed out sensibly. "Dogs don't eat cookies."

"Baby does," Charlie said, shouldering her way to the front so she could see Colt better.

"Only when you give them to her," Colt reminded her with a smile. He glanced at Tommy who was fidgeting in his wheelchair. "Tommy, do you have to go to the bathroom?" he asked suspiciously.

"He always gots to go to the bathroom," Charlie said with a quick roll of her eyes.

"Tommy?" Colt looked at him.

The blond head nodded solemnly.

"Then go." Colt turned and pushed his bathroom door open wider. Luckily, the house had been built years ago, and had extra wide doorways long before they'd become fashionable or mandatory to accommodate wheelchairs. "You need any help?" Colt called.

"I'm four," Tommy said, clearly insulted. "I could go to the bathroom by myself."

"Okay," Colt said, turning back to the expectant faces. "You're here because of cookies. Have I got that much so far?"

Three heads nodded in unison.

"Good." He grinned, shifting Mary Sunshine in his arms. "Now what about cookies?"

Charlie and Eddy exchanged glances, as if deciding who was going to ask. Charlie nudged Eddie aside, stepping forward. "It's Saturday," she began, eyes pleading. "And it's gonna be Christmas on Friday."

He tried not to wince at the mention of the holiday. The closer it got, the more claustrophobic he felt.

"Okay, Charlie, it's Saturday, and Friday is...I got it." Colt nodded. "So what does that have to do with cookies?"

"You don't got to go to work today, do you?" Charlie's gaze searched his, and he knew whatever they wanted—needed was obviously important.

He bent down until he was eye level with her. "Well, I'm the sheriff, honey, I've always got to go to work, but if you need me for something, I'm sure I can spare a few hours." He'd already rearranged the duty schedule so he'd be home early this afternoon for the kids first riding lesson. From the looks of things, he was going to have to do a little more rearranging.

"Good." She beamed at him as the trio clapped their hands in glee. Never had one word had such an ominous reaction.

Colt looked first at Charlie, and then at each of the kids in turn, wondering if he was about to be conned by a group of ragtag moppets.

"Good?" One brow rose. "Why is that good?" he asked, looking from one to the other.

"'Cuz today is cookie Saturday," they caroled in unison, squealing in delight, obviously thrilled.

Colt blinked in confusion. "What?" He looked from one to the other. "It's *what* kind of Saturday?"

"Cookie Saturday," Eddy repeated, shouldering Charlie over so he could speak—man to man again—with Colt. "Sadie said it's a Blackwell family tradition to bake Christmas cookies on the Saturday before Christmas."

Miraculously, Colt held back a groan. He was well aware of almost all of Sadie's traditions. He'd spent a lifetime avoiding them.

"Yeth," Mary Sunshine put in, pressing her nose against his cheek. "And we want you to make cookies with us. Can you? Can you? Pease?"

"Make cookies?" he said weakly. "You want me to make cookies?"

"Christmas cookies," Charlie specified lest there was any confusion. She reached for his hand, tugged it in a pleading gesture. "Please Colt, make cookies with us? We're gonna make special ones just for Santa."

"For...Santa?" Colt repeated weakly. Three heads bobbed up and down again.

"Santa's got to have something to eat," Eddy blinked owlishly at him. "And we're gonna make him cookies." Eddy crossed his arms across his skinny chest as if the matter was settled. "We want you to help."

Colt nodded. He'd gotten that part. And he was absolutely certain he'd rather have his eyes ripped out with fishhooks. But looking at the hopeful faces peering up at him, he didn't have the heart to turn them down.

Not without feeling like a heel.

"Cookies, huh?" His gaze went from one expectant face to the other. Three heads nodded in unison, giving him a sad, sinking feeling in his gut.

"Yeth, for Santa." Mary Sunshine kissed his cheek, winding her arms tighter around him. "P...pease? P...ease help? We'll be good. Pwomise."

Her words tugged at his heart. "Honey, you guys are always good," he said with a reassuring smile, planting a kiss on her cheek.

"And we won't feed any to Baby." Charlie grinned, slinging a skinny arm around Eddy's shoulders in a gesture of solidarity. "Right?"

"Right," they crowed, grinning with youthful enthusiasm, and more than a little mischief.

"I'm sure Sadie will appreciate that," Colt said

mildly. Obviously, Baby's diet and digestion had already been a hot topic of discussion, one he was glad he had missed.

"So, does that mean you'll help?" Eddy asked, looking up at him hopefully.

Colt let his gaze drift from one adorable face to another. How on earth could anyone deny these kids—any kids—anything, he wondered.

"Guess it does at that," he said with a reluctant smile, starting a round of cheering. He sighed. So he'd rearrange his schedule once again. And hope like hell he'd be able to get through the morning. Cookies, he thought with another sigh. Christmas cookies no less.

"He'ths gonna help us," Mary squealed as Tommy wheeled back in the room.

"Told you." Grinning, Tommy wheeled closer to beam up at Colt.

Colt nodded. "But no cookie baking until after breakfast," Colt specified, carefully setting Mary Sunshine back down on her feet, holding onto her until he was certain she had her balance. "And I've got some ground rules," he said as he straightened.

"Rules?" Eddy looked dubious. "What kind of rules, sir?" he asked suspiciously.

"No cookie baking until I've had some coffee."

Eddie considered for a moment, then he shrugged. "Okay."

"Are you going to bake cookies in your bathrobe?" Charlie wanted to know making him laugh.

"Uh, no, you guys scram so I can get dressed."

He glanced at the clock on his bureau as he opened the door, surprised to find Brenna standing there with a grin on her face. He smiled back at her before turning back to the kids. "Give me ten minutes and I'll meet you in the kitchen."

"Don't be late," Charlie ordered, as she shepherded the group out of his room and toward the kitchen.

"Christmas cookies?" Brenna asked with an amused lift of her brow as she leaned against the doorjamb. She wasn't going to let the surprise show on her face. She was far too touched by his gesture, knowing how much he'd kept insisting he didn't "do" Christmas. Apparently for the children, he was willing to "do" anything.

"For Santa," he said with a dismal nod of his head.

"I see." She was trying so hard not to grin, but couldn't hold it in. "I...I...uh, came looking for them. When I found their beds were empty, I figured they were here."

"They conned me," he admitted. "They ambushed me and took me by surprise."

"Uh-huh." She stepped forward, laid a hand on his shoulders and planted a soft kiss on his mouth. "You, Colt Blackwell, are a fake." She kissed him again. "A big unbelievable phony."

He sighed, then kissed her back. "Yeah," he grumbled, drawing her deeper into the room and into his arms before kicking the door shut, knowing he only had ten minutes. But he planned to make the best of it. "Just don't let it get around," he murmured as he lowered his mouth to hers once again.

"Colt, what are you doing?" She slapped his hands away and continued to mix Sadie's famous bread pudding recipe. "It's Christmas Eve, I've got a million things left to do, and I really don't have time for nonsense."

She didn't mean to be short, but he'd been making himself scarce—again—the entire week, and now he'd burst into the kitchen, demanding she go with him…somewhere—he hadn't bothered to specify exactly where.

Obviously, the man was oblivious to the fact that Christmas Eve warranted more than a little extra attention, especially when you were responsible for six small, nearly giddy-with-anticipation munchkins.

"Nonsense?" One brow rose and Colt shook his head, reaching for the wooden spoon, slipping it from her hands and ignoring her squeak of outrage. Anticipation was racing through him as he reached for her again. "I've seen nonsense, Doc, and trust me this isn't it."

"But Colt—"

"Now," he said as he reached around her, untied her apron, then took her arm, turning her toward the back door. "This can't wait." Without giving her another chance to protest, he hustled her out the back door, down the driveway and toward his car.

"But what about Sadie's bread pudding?" she

asked with a frown, turning to glance back at the house.

"Trust me, Sadie can handle bread pudding and anything else thrown at her. She's a pro."

"How long is this going to take?" Brenna asked, pushing a lock of hair off her cheek as she climbed into the car. "I put the kids down for a nap otherwise by dinner they'd all be wound up tighter than drums. And tonight's a big night for them. Not to mention a late night." She glanced back at the house, thinking about all of the things she still had left to do.

She continued to stare out the window, her mind mulling over the mental list of things still left undone. "I don't like leaving Sadie all alone with them," she finally said, chewing her lip.

With a laugh, Colt pulled out of the driveway, taking the road that would lead them through and out of town. He tried not to scowl at the array of decorations adorning every house in sight, and instead concentrated on the road.

The closer the holiday came, the worse his claustrophobia got. He knew he couldn't hang on much longer; he was going to have to bolt if he wanted to hang on to his sanity.

He'd managed to handle the cooking-baking-caper, but it had been close. Real close. Leaving him shaky and surly. That, coupled with all the other hoopla that was going on in preparation for the holiday was making his feet antsy to move.

But he wanted this taken care of now. For Brenna. For the kids.

Then he could take off for a few days with a clear conscience and lick his wounds in private.

But not until he took care of this one last task.

''Sadie's the last person you need to worry about when it comes to those kids. She loves having them here and I can assure you from experience, she can handle anything, including six wild, wound-up kids.''

''Sadie's wonderful with them,'' Brenna admitted with a smile. ''So is Endy, but I don't want to take advantage of them.'' She folded her hands in her lap so she wouldn't reach out and touch him. Touching him had become so...ordinary, necessary. She couldn't even remember when he wasn't a part of her—and the kids'—daily life.

''They've helped so much, what with the kids' daily tutoring, their physical exercises, and all the extra work that's required because of the kids' special needs.'' Her voice trailed off. ''The kids are really going to miss everyone when it's time to leave.'' She had put off thinking about leaving the Blackwell's home, leaving Colt simply because she couldn't bear to think of him not being in her—their life.

She'd done the unthinkable, she realized, still looking at him. She'd fallen in love with him.

And for the life of her, she hadn't a clue what to do about it. There was nerves, and fear, of course, unbelievable fear, particularly knowing that the time to leave his home, and his...care was fast approaching, and that meant, he would probably no longer be part of her daily life. She simply couldn't bear to think about it, not knowing how she'd survive without him in her life.

"We're here." Colt came to a stop, shut off the car, and turned to her. "Welcome home, Brenna," he said softly.

Blinking, she turned, and her eyes widened. "Colt?" she breathed, her hand going to her mouth.

"It's finished. All the renovations, all the repairs, everything is done. Bill Powers, the building inspector made a special trip out here this morning to make certain everything was up to code." He hopped out and came around to open her door, taking her hand to help her out. "I even hassled Mr. Wallace and got him to come out this morning and give the place a once-over, and his seal of approval. So you're fully legal and can move back in tonight. Just in time for...well, just like I promised."

Stunned, Brenna merely stood still, staring at the Home. Her home. The Children's Home.

Tears filled her eyes. "It's so...beautiful." She shook her head, certain she must be dreaming. "I simply can't believe it," she said, as he took her hand and led her toward the glistening new oak front door. Grinning at her pleased expression, Colt extracted a brand new shiny key and handed it to her.

"Would you like to do the honors?"

Still feeling as if she was in a daze, Brenna looked at him, then down at the key, then back up at him, a ghost of a grin playing around her lips. It broke loose, and she slid the key into the lock and threw open the door. Her breath came out in a rush.

"Oh my." She stepped inside, her hand at her pounding heart. A mixture of scents assaulted her. The smell of new furniture. The pungent scent of fresh paint, as well as the acid scent of varnish and carpenter's glue, but she was certain she'd never smelled anything more wonderful. "Oh my," she said again, turning in a circle, trying to take everything in at once.

Colt reached for her hand. "Just about everything is new."

"I can see that," she said with a laugh, letting him lead her down the newly widened carpeted hallway, glancing at the almost invisible sliding doors that led to the elevator. "It doesn't even look like the same place." Her gaze raced around the rooms. "But how...how did you manage to pay for all of this? Surely the Home's insurance wasn't this...extravagant?"

"We used the money my folks had raised for the renovations until the insurance money came through," he said, leading her from room to room. Each room was more beautiful than the last. "It was tight for a while, but luckily I've got good credit." He tugged her through another doorway. "Come see your new office."

She came to a halt. "Colt, you didn't use *your* money for this?" she asked horrified.

With a laugh, he shook his head. "Nope. Not a

penny.'' He held up his free hand. ''Honest. When the insurance company was dragging their feet, Cutter sicced my dad on them, my dad made a few calls, and the next thing I knew, Wallace called and said the check was in.''

Until then, most of the building merchants had agreed to give him the materials he needed just on his signature, but he saw no point in telling Brenna that. She'd just worry about it, and besides, every penny had been repaid now, so there was no point in going through the logistics.

''This...this is my office?'' Brenna walked around the newly expanded, expansive room, running her hand over the brand new oak desk.

The walls were painted a cheery yellow, but were minus all of her diplomas, which had been destroyed in the fire; instead, the walls were decorated with gaily crayon-colored pictures.

''Do you like it?'' Colt asked.

''I love it,'' she admitted, taking in the neat new row of filing cabinets. A small oak credenza and matching bookcases that adorned one wall. Taking a step closer, Brenna looked at the pictures. ''Did the kids draw those?'' she asked in surprise, turning to him.

His grin widened. ''You didn't see those yet.'' He held a hand in front of her eyes, deliberately spreading his fingers so she could see through them. ''They're supposed to be a surprise. Come on, let's go see the kitchen, and then we'll go upstairs, I want you to see all the bedrooms.''

He led her from room to room. The kitchen had been expanded, and renovated. A long, low deacon's table, with two long and extrawide benches with supporting backs sat on either side.

Sparkling new, oversized appliances with safety features adorned the cheery azure room. A huge bay window, with several shelves for growing herbs or plants and a perfect view of the expansive grounds sat over the sink.

Still holding her hand, Colt led her upstairs and through the bedrooms. Each room had been designed and equipped with the paraphernalia necessary to accommodate the kids' needs. Wide doorways with sleek new banisters ran around each wall. Wide shower stalls had low-hung handrails. Sinks were set lower to the ground, some with pull-out stools for sitting.

Matching cherry bedroom sets filled four of the bedrooms Each held a pair of beds that had a pair of hideaway rails for safety, as well as small, secure self-enclosed two-step ladders with handrails so the kids could get themselves in and out of bed without fear of falling.

The windows had all been replaced and no longer whistled with the wind. Although they were bare now, they allowed a view of the extensive grounds.

Nearly overwhelmed, tears welled again and she threw herself at Colt, hugging him tight.

"Colt, I don't know what to say." She had to swallow the lump in her throat. It was like a dream come true, knowing the kids would have a beautiful home, and beautiful bedrooms to call their own. "Or how to thank you."

Wrapping his arms around her waist, he held her, savoring her scent. "I think you're saying it pretty well." He pressed a kiss to her forehead. "I was a little worried we wouldn't finish on time, but everyone hustled their butts and—"

She drew back and looked at him, loving shining in her eyes, echoing in her heart. "You did this for Charlie, didn't you?" she asked softly, laying a hand to his cheek. "Because you promised she'd be home for Christmas."

He shifted uncomfortably. "I did it for all the kids, Brenna. And you." He pressed a kiss to her mouth, pleased at the pleasure he saw reflected in her eyes.

"The kids will be so excited." She laughed, spinning around in a circle. "There's only one thing missing."

"What?" he repeated, glancing around wondering what he'd forgotten.

"A Christmas tree—"

"Nope," he said with a grin. "It's already taken care of." Colt glanced at his watch. "Hunter's out buying a tree now. He should be here any minute. I figured you and the kids would want to decorate the tree yourself." He turned her by the shoulders. "See that door over there at the end of the hall?"

"Yeah?"

"It's just one of six storage rooms. You'll have plenty of room to store any and everything. You'll find some new ornaments in there, for your tree, courtesy of Sadie. She went shopping yesterday, and I think she bought out every store in Blackwell." He grinned sheepishly at the look on her face. "Sadie figured you and the kids would want to decorate a tree in your new home."

She wound her arms around him. "She figured right." Pressing her lips to his, she smiled.

"Uh...Brenna, I know you think the kids are napping—"

"Think?" She gave him a measured look. "They're not napping?" she asked and he laughed.

"Not a chance. Cutter's supervising them. Honest. They're packing up their things so that they can move back here tonight, just in time for..." He couldn't say it. He simply couldn't. "Anyway, the whole family will be here in about an hour to help get you settled in."

The way he said it caused a warning bell to go off. "And what about you, Colt? Are you going to help us get settled?" She watched his face change, darken. Saw a muscle in his jaw tense.

"I've...I've...got some things to take care of," he said.

"I see." She tried not to let it hurt. It was Christmas Eve after all. Naturally he had some things to do. "How...how long will these...things take?"

Dragging a hand through his hair, he avoided looking at her. There was pure hurt in her eyes.

"I don't know." He shrugged. "I figure I should be back within a week. Maybe two." By then he hoped to have gotten himself together, and more importantly, be over the worst of it.

He never wanted her to know. Never wanted her to see that he was a coward, that he couldn't face the present, not with the blistering memories of his past.

He'd managed to hold everything together this long simply because of her, and the kids, simply to keep his promise to Charlie because she'd depended on him.

But he wasn't sure how much longer he could hold things back. Or in. Especially now.

Realization dawned slowly. "You're leaving?" Brenna struggled to keep the tears at bay. "You won't be here for...Christmas?"

"Never planned on being here." Her face had drained, her eyes had gone glassy with tears. He was certain something was ripping apart inside of him.

Now that the Home was completed, a task that had occupied his time and his mind, he found that all the emotions he'd hidden and buried were threatening to unleash, and he couldn't let them, not now, not yet.

Not here in front of her. He needed to be alone.

"You look surprised." He couldn't keep the annoyance out of his voice, knowing he was more annoyed with himself, for hurting her, for disappointing her than with anything else.

She had to swallow the lump in her throat. It was only by extreme effort that kept her tears from falling. ''I...guess I am surprised.'' She dared a glance at him. ''It *is* Christmas Eve.''

''So? What about it?'' He looked at her carefully, then dawning horror had his voice rising. ''Don't tell me you thought I was going to play Santa Claus?''

The memories had started to come back, to flood his mind, and drown his empty, barren heart. And he knew he simply couldn't handle it, not with his emotions in such turmoil over her. His history had been etched in stone long before he'd ever fallen in love with a beautiful doc, and her adorable group of ragtag kids.

He couldn't change the present unless he could change his past. And his belief in miracles had burned to death on a bitterly cold Christmas Eve night so many years ago.

''You had no right,'' he charged, his voice gruff and rising. ''I told you the day we met that I wouldn't do it, didn't I?''

''Yes,'' she whispered in a ragged voice. ''You told me.''

Fists clenched at his side in frustration, he took a step closer. ''I told you to hire someone to play Santa, didn't I?''

''Y...yes, but I thought—''

''You had no right to think anything. I never lied to you, Brenna. I never promised you or the kids anything.''

''No, Sheriff, you didn't.'' Inhaling a slow, calming breath, Brenna leveled her chin. ''You never promised us anything.'' The tone of her voice was so heartbreakingly detached, so cool and calm, he wanted to punch a wall in frustration.

He'd hurt her, he knew it, but there wasn't anything he could do about it. Not now. His mind told him to run; his heart urged him to stay. He wanted to grab her close, to hold her, to tell her everything he'd held inside for so many years, but he couldn't. He didn't know if he could face the horror of the truth, so how could he expect her too?

"I never lied to you, Brenna,'' he repeated, wondering why he felt the need to defend himself. "I told you to hire someone, and if you didn't, it's your own fault.''

Brenna took a slow, careful breath. He was turning his back on her, blaming her, the same way her husband had done to ease his own conscience when he'd done something hurtful.

She would not answer him, she decided, nor would she explain, for she knew any explanation she gave would seem inadequate, especially since any explanation would make it clear she was in love with him. Something she couldn't tell him, not now.

She would never admit that she was in love with him, and being in love had made her believe—in miracles. She'd felt certain that since he'd gotten to know her, gotten to know the children, he'd have changed his mind.

Apparently she'd been wrong.

"Why didn't you hire someone?'' he demanded,

grabbing her shoulders, frustration and pain eating at him. The kids were going to be hugely disappointed, and it was his fault. He knew it. He'd unknowingly let them down because Brenna had assumed he'd changed his mind.

To agree to play Santa meant he'd have to stick around, have to endure and participate in the holiday, have to remember, over and over again, remember the night he'd tried so hard to forget for so many years.

He couldn't do it. He simply couldn't do it.

"You had no right to assume that I had changed my mind. We never discussed this, Brenna. Never. I told you that I wouldn't do it." She'd never know how much this pained him, never know that his control was hanging on by a thin, fragile thread.

She bit her lip, refusing to cry. But his words had carved a crater-size hole in her heart. She'd trusted him, believed in him, simply because she'd fallen in love with him. Worse, she'd let the children fall in love with him, an even more unpardonable sin.

They were going to be hurt. Heartbroken she realized. And it was all her fault. She was the adult, she knew better, was supposed to understand emotions and relationship. At the moment, she wasn't certain she understood anything.

All she knew was that no matter what the kids were going to be hurt. And she had let it happen when she *knew* better.

She chose her words carefully. "Thank you for

all you've done for me, for the children, but I think perhaps you should leave."

"You want me to leave?" He glared at her for a long moment with eyes that were so bleak and cold, she wanted to weep. "Fine! I'm outta here." Turning on his heel, he stormed down the stairs and down the hallway.

It wasn't until Brenna heard the front door slam with a shudder, that she sank to the floor and let the tears of heartbreak free.

"You're silly, Ma," Charlie said with a quick roll of her eyes as she bounced up and down on her new bed. "Course Santa's going come. He can find us. We're home." Charlie stifled a huge yawn, then slid under the covers. Taking her glasses off, she set them on the bedside table.

Brenna sighed, stroking a hand over her daughter's head as she tucked her in. Not wanting the kids to be unprepared, as well as disappointed, she'd tried to explain that this year, Santa might not come.

But the kids weren't having any of it. They still believed, believed in Santa, believed in miracles, Christmas miracles, and Brenna had no idea how on earth she was going to tell them the truth, knowing it was going to break their hearts.

"Good night, sweetie." Brushing her lips against Charlie's forehead, Brenna flipped on the nightlight. "I'll see you in the morning."

"Night, Ma." Charlie yawned again, snuggling further under the covers. "Merry Christmas."

Her eyes were dry now, but a lump seemed permanently lodged in her throat. ''Merry Christmas, sweetheart.''

Brenna rose, and went to tuck Mary Sunshine's arms under the covers. She gave Mary a soft kiss, then turned on her night light. ''Sleep tight, kids.'' With one last final look, she slipped out of the room.

The house was still and silent. All of the other kids were sound asleep already. Brenna actually looked forward to the hours and hours of work that lay ahead now that the kids were asleep, certain that with all the excitement of getting the kids moved back in and settled, coupled with decorating the new Christmas tree, and now, assembling toys and wrapping packages, not to mention setting the table for Christmas breakfast, by the time she actually went to bed, she'd be too tired to think.

All of the Blackwells, well all except for Colt were coming to share Christmas dinner with them, including Justin and Emma Blackwell who'd arrived from Florida earlier in the evening. It was going to be a real family Christmas for the children, surrounded by their newfound extended family, a family who loved and accepted them for who they were.

Brenna should have been thrilled.

Instead, she was simply miserable.

''Ma, Ma, wake up!'' Charlie was bouncing on the bed, shaking her. ''Santa's here! Santa's here!''

Rubbing the sleep out of her eyes, Brenna reached

out a hand to stop Charlie's bouncing. It was making her nauseous.

"W-what?" Brenna pushed the hair out of her eyes and sat up, blinking hard. "What did you say, Charlie?" She'd lain awake most of the night, crying, dozing off right after the sun rose, which seemed about three minutes ago. Now, her eyes felt as if someone had sprinkled sand into them.

"Santa's here." Charlie turned toward the door. "Listen!" Charlie started bouncing again. "I told ya, Ma. I told ya."

"Charlie, I know you probably think that Santa—" Brenna stopped, then listened for a moment. "What on earth?" The deep rumble of a male voice had her grabbing her robe with one hand, and Charlie with the other. "Where's the rest of the kids?" Brenna asked in alarm as she stuffed her arms into her robe.

"Downstairs with Santa," Charlie said with a huge grin, tugging her mother's hand to get her moving. "I told ya, Ma."

"Yes, you did," Brenna murmured, wondering what was going on. "But you know you're not supposed to go downstairs without me."

"But it's Christmas," Charlie said by way of explanation, tugging Brenna's hand as she led her slowly down the stairs. "And we didn't want to miss Santa."

"Charlie, I don't know what's—"

"Ho! Ho! Ho! So who's this pretty little lady?"

Brenna's eyes widened as she took in...Santa

Claus? Maybe she was dreaming. She peered closer. No, it wasn't a dream, but a distinct reality.

"Santa?" she said hesitantly, drawing her robe closer around her.

"You got a good eye, Doc," Santa announced with a wink, leaving her mouth hanging open, and her heart…soaring. Beard, wig, pillow stuffed in his pants or not, she'd recognize that voice, those eyes anywhere.

Colt.

"W-what…" She had to press a hand to her mouth and start over. "What are you doing here, Santa?"

"It's Christmas, Ma," Charlie said with a quick roll of her eyes. "Where else would Santa be?"

"We fed him cookies," Mary Sunshine announced, grabbing Santa's hand and staring up at him with open admiration. "Didn't we?"

Santa swung her up in his arms, nuzzling her. "You sure did, Sunshine."

"And they were good, too, right Santa?" Eddy the Boss asked, trying to appear grown-up, but grinning all the same.

"The bestest," Tommy announced, wheeling his chair closer to get a better look Santa. "Right?"

Santa ruffled his blond hair. "You got that right, son." Santa rubbed his tummy. "I ate them all up."

Brenna couldn't stop staring at him.

Santa swung Mary to one hip, then dug into a large white bag that was on the floor. "Now, let's see what we've got." He lifted a gaily wrapped present from the bag, and pretended to read it. "Anyone here named...Bubkus?"

"Bubkus isn't a kid," Charlie announced with a scowl. "It's Mikey's frog."

"A frog, huh?" Santa pretended to peer closer at the present. "Oh, yeah, guess this one goes to...Charlie then."

With a squeal, Charlie pounced on the gift, tearing the paper open with relish. She let out a squeal as she lifted out a six-pack of nail polish in various shades of shocking red. "More nail polish." She lifted it in the air. "And lipsticks. Lots and lots of red lipsticks."

"Wonderful," Brenna said dully, giving Santa a scowl.

"Something wrong there, Doc?" Santa asked with a twinkle in his eye.

"Nothing." She couldn't contain her grin. "Nothing at all."

"Good." Santa lifted another present out of the bag. "Anyone here named...Tommy?" Santa glanced around as if not sure who Tommy was.

"That's me! That's me!" Wheeling his chair closer, Tommy snatched the present from Santa's hands.

"Leave the fingers, boy," Santa said with a laugh. "I might need them later."

"It's gloves," Tommy said, holding up his present.

"Riding gloves," Santa specified, hunkering down so he was eye level with the boy. "Heard you were worried you wouldn't be able to learn to ride a horse like the rest of the kids, but Santa doesn't think it will be a problem.'' He met Brenna's gaze over the top of Tommy's head. The look in his eyes warmed her heart. ''With a few adjustments, you can ride just like all the other kids.'' Santa nodded toward the gift. ''Thought you should have some gloves to protect your hands, though.''

''Really?'' Tommy's eyes widened in joy as he stared at Santa, then his gloves, then back again. He swung his chair around and aimed for Charlie. ''Guess what? Santa says I could ride a horse.''

''Okay, kids, this one's for Mikey the Mischief Maker and Petey.'' Santa glanced around. ''Are they here?''

''I'm here,'' a little cross-eyed redheaded moppet said. ''I'm Petey,'' he said with a toothless grin. He grabbed the leg of Santa's pants, tugging him downward so he could whisper something in his ear.

Santa's eyes widened, and his gaze went to Brenna's, then he laughed, ruffling the redhead's hair.

''Okay, son, I get the picture. Until Mikey's... rounded up the wayward critters, you can do the honors.'' Santa started to set the long, square box into the boy's arms, but hesitated. ''Now, Petey, this present is real special. You and Mikey have to promise to take care of this together.''

''We will,'' the little redhead said with a solemn nod. ''We'll take reallllllll good care of it.''

''Now, you've got to open this present carefully

so you don't scare it," Santa said as he set the box in the boy's arms.

"Scare it?" Brenna said in alarm, taking a step closer. Her gaze flew to Colt's—Santa. "What's...in there that Petey might scare?"

"It's a snake," Petey said in awe, looking at the clear glass box with the spring-locked lid top. "A real snake."

Brenna's stomach flipped. Several times. "A...a snake?" One brow lifted and she tried to glare at Santa, but one look at Petey's face, and she couldn't manage it.

"It's a ball python," Santa said more to Brenna than to Tommy."

"A...python," she stammered.

Santa grinned, then rubbed his beard. "Yeah, his name's Monti."

"Monti Python?" Brenna asked incredulously.

Santa nodded. "He's not poisonous, Doc, but you've got to make sure you lock the top. He's only a couple of months old, but in another month or so he'll be strong enough to push the top off and get loose."

"Loose?" Brenna said weakly, glancing back at the clear box with a sense of dread.

"He's gonna keep Bubkus company." Engrossed in his newest pet, Petey carried to box to a corner and sat down, anxious to show the other kids who crowded around him for a look at their first ever real honest-to-goodness snake.

Santa pulled another gaily wrapped present out of his bag. "Looks like this one's for Mary Sunshine."

"That's me." Eyes shining, Mary started bouncing on her tiptoes, reaching for her gift. "That's me. That's me." Slow, she tore open the wrapper, then squealed. "It's a doll." She hugged it close to her heart. "And look, she wears glasses just like us."

Santa dug into his bag again, pretending to squint to read the name. "This one's for Mr. Boss. Mr. Edward Boss." He glanced around, and over Eddy's head.

"That's me, sir, Santa." Eddy swallowed, waiting patiently for Santa to look at him.

"Ah, here you are, son." Santa handed over the present. "Careful now, it's heavy."

Juggling it carefully, Eddy slowly, meticulously opened his present. "It's a chemistry set," he exclaimed, his eyes wide with joy. "Look, Brenna. Look! A real chemistry set. Now I can mix things, and experiment."

"Wonderful," Brenna said weakly. "Maybe you can experiment on how to get rid of snakes."

"Uh...Doc." Santa was holding another present in his hand. "Looks like this one's for you."

"For me?" Brenna asked in surprise. Hesitantly, she reached out and took the small, brightly wrapped package as Santa stepped closer.

She glanced up at him, then slowly, carefully ripped open the present. Her heart started pounding when she saw the small, black box. Her hands were trembling when she opened it.

"Colt—" she breathed. The ring was beautiful. It had a perfectly round-cut center diamond, surrounded by six smaller diamonds.

"Will you marry me, Brenna?" He took her hand in his, realizing how scared he was, how much this meant to him, how much she meant to him. He'd spent a torturous night, trying to live down his memories, only to realize that the pain of losing Brenna and the kids far overshadowed the pain of anything from his past.

That's when he realized perhaps it was time to face his fears, and his memories. To face them, and then to put them away for good. In the past, where they belonged. It was finally time for Colt to have a future, a future he wanted to share with Brenna and the kids.

"I know I've got a lot of explaining to do. It won't be easy, but I realized last night that it's time to put the past behind me. I'm ready to move forward, to plan a future, with you, and with the kids."

Brenna shook her head, not certain she wasn't dreaming. "Marry you?" Brenna breathed, her heart leaping in joy.

"We're going to have to get your hearing checked, Doc," he teased, leaning close to speak directly into her startled face. "Yes, I want you to marry me. All of you." Colt said, slipping his arm around her as the kids, aware that something was going on, crowded around, wide-eyed.

Colt pointed to the ring. "See, there's one large diamond in the center, that one's for you, Doc. And then there's six small ones, one for each of the kids. Our kids, Brenna. Yours and mine, if you all will have me."

"Oh Colt," she whispered, laying her head to his chest with a relieved sigh. She loved him so much. And he loved her. And all the kids. No matter what terrors or demons they had to face, they'd face them together. As a family. As it should be.

Perhaps there were Christmas miracles after all.

"I want you all to marry me, Brenna." His gaze slowly traveled to each adorable face. "So what do you say, kids, do you want to marry me?"

The kids exchanged silent glances, and then Charlie called them into a huddle, where they exchanged hurried whispers, much to Brenna and Colt's surprise.

When they broke, Charlie came to the forefront to announce their decision. "Santa, we're sorry, we love you, and you give good presents, but we want to marry Colt."

"Yeth," Mary Sunshine chimed in, still hugging her doll tight. "We want to marry Colt. We love him and he makes real good cookies."

"And he loves us," Tommy interjected, wheeling up and almost over Santa's toes.

"Thank you, Santa sir." Always the gentlemen, Eddy the Boss reached for Santa's hand and gave it a hearty shake. "But we can't marry you."

Banking down a smile, Colt nodded, then swung his bag over his shoulder. "Guess that's settled then." He couldn't resist, he pressed a kiss to

Brenna's temple, then whispered in her ear. "I'll be back in a few minutes."

"Are you sure?" she asked, still holding the ring.

"Positive." He kissed her again, slipping the ring on her finger. "Don't go away." He winked. "I'll be right back."

"I wouldn't dream of it." Her eyes were swimming with joy, her heart bursting with love.

"I love you, Brenna."

"I love you, too, Colt—Santa."

"Bye Santa," the kids caroled, trooping along after him toward the door.

"Merry Christmas," Santa called with a hearty wave.

"Merry Christmas," the kids caroled back, small hands waving fiercely as they watched Santa slip out the door.

"All right, kids, everyone upstairs to get dressed for breakfast before Sadie and Endy, and everyone else arrives for dinner.

For a brief moment, Colt turned and glanced back at the loving faces of the children, and at Brenna, and his heart overflowed with love. He knew he had some explaining to do, but he had no doubt that no matter what he and Brenna could work anything out.

Now he realized that was what love and Christmas were all about.

"I was eight, and Cade was three," Colt said while the kids were upstairs dressing. He and Brenna had curled up on the couch in front of the fireplace amidst a pile of Christmas wrapping paper, and the soft whisper of Christmas carols playing softly through the new intercom system.

He'd decided the time was right to tell her, to share with her his past, so that they could all share a future.

"We were close. Real close. I looked after him, took care of him. He was just...a little tyke." He had to take a deep breath.

"Colt, where were your parents?" Brenna asked softly.

"Parents?" Colt laughed, but the sound held no mirth. "My old man had split long before that. As for my mother..." His voice trailed off and he shook his head, not certain he could even speak of the woman who had the audacity to call herself a mother.

"My mother." He shook his head. "She couldn't have cared less about me or Cade. We lived in a run-down walk-up on the other side of Blackwell, in a two-room apartment with barely enough heat or electricity. She didn't care much for taking care of us. As long as she had a bottle, and her men friends, she was happy." Colt took a long, slow breath. "That Christmas Eve, I went out and bought a Christmas tree. It was the first tree the kid—Cade had ever seen. That tree was practically dead, but the guy on the corner who was selling them let me have it for shoveling his walk because it was Christmas Eve." He smiled suddenly.

"I found some old ornaments and lights up in the

attic, and we decorated the tree. You should have seen Cade's face when I turned those lights on." He laughed softly, the remembered pleasure so strong it warmed him.

For the first time in more years than he could remember, he allowed himself to think of Cade. To remember. In an instant, Cade's face, sweet and innocent floated through Colt's mind. It had been so long since he'd allowed himself to think about Cade, or to speak about him that now he simply smiled in remembered pleasure, and love, and the pain seemed to ease.

"I wanted the kid to have a real Christmas like other kids, you know. I'd shoveled snow all winter to save up enough money to buy him a present. He always talked about being a sheriff, so I bought him a little silver sheriff's badge for Christmas."

"That night, Christmas Eve, my ma went out as usual." With his free hand, he rubbed his eyes. "Those old lights caught fire."

"Oh God." Brenna clutched his shirt, burying her face in his chest, holding onto him.

"I couldn't get to Cade. He was in his crib across the room. Something woke me up. I smelled the smoke, saw it slithering under the door like an insidious snake. I panicked. I couldn't get free."

Her head lifted. "Free? What do you mean free?"

"Whenever my mother went out, she tied us to our beds. I'd learned how to get loose, and then tie myself back up before she ever got home. But that night..." His voice trailed off for a moment and he had to swallow again. "That night I was so scared, so panicked because of the fire, I couldn't get my bindings loose. Cade woke up and started crying. Hearing his cries only made my panic deepen. I had to get free so I could get to him, to untie him and get him out of that inferno. But I couldn't. I was too panicked, too scared."

Horrified, Brenna could no longer hold back her tears and let them slide quietly down her cheeks. "Oh Colt." She clung to him, feeling a rush of emotions, a rush of love so strong it nearly overwhelmed her.

"He was depending on me, Brenna. Cade was just a little kid and I let him down."

"Oh Colt." Gently, she turned his head toward her, her heart breaking at what she saw in his eyes, at what he'd gone through, what he'd done to himself. "So that's why you hate Christmas?"

"Hated Christmas," he corrected with a smile, picking up her hand to lace his fingers through hers. "It's past tense." He dragged her closer, kissing her hair, lifting her hand where the ring he'd given her sparkled in the darkness. "You and those kids, I didn't realize how much or how powerful love is, Brenna." He looked into her eyes. "Not until I met you did I realize that love has the power to heal." He smiled at her. "I guess my heart was so caught up in you and the kids, my mind so preoccupied, I didn't realize until last night that all the memories I'd been fighting to banish, that I thought I had to run away from had been replaced by memories of you.'' He blew out a breath. ''When you asked me to leave, I thought the world had come to an end. At least my world. And I knew then that I was in love with you—with all of you. If I wanted to have a future, I had to settle with my past. I've never talked about this with anyone, not ever, but telling you about it, talking about it now seems to have released the pain, the guilt I carried for so long.''

''I understand.'' She snuggled closer, kissing his chin. ''I love you.''

''I love you, too. You and the kids have filled the hole in my heart with love.'' He lifted her hand, and touched the ring she now wore on her hand. His ring—his wife. ''I guess like this ring, my life has finally come full circle.

''Our life,'' she corrected with a smile. ''Together.''

The sound of the kids chattering and clamoring filtered down the stairs.

Colt glanced up. ''Sounds like the munchkins are restless,'' he said with a laugh.

''Well, it *is* Christmas, Colt.'' She kissed him.

''Yeah, it is.'' He drew her to her feet. ''Well, Doc, what do you say we go celebrate Christmas?'' He kissed her hand. ''Together.''

She laughed, joy filling her heart. ''Sounds like a plan to me.''

He drew her into his arms. ''Definitely a plan. For this Christmas and every one to come.''

She threw her arms around him, her heart bursting with joy. ''I love you, Colt Blackwell. I love you.''

She kissed him again. "And no matter what the future holds, we'll face it together. All of us. The way it should be."

"Agreed." He kissed her again as the fire crackled quietly. "I love you, Brenna." His mouth captured hers, as he hauled her closer, pressing close to her, wanting to absorb the heat, the life and love of her.

Where once he would have run, his heart, now healed, held him there with love.

With love.

Epilogue

The Home was finally quiet except for the crackling of the fire in the fireplace. The heavenly scents from dinner, courtesy of Sadie, still wafted through the air.

The tree was lit, winking on and off in a soft cacophony of lights. The new color television flickered softly from across the room.

The children, exhausted from the day's activities were sprawled in assorted chairs and on the floor.

Exhausted as well, Baby lay snoring quietly in front of the fireplace. Atop her head, and entwined around her big, floppy ears was a gaily tied red ribbon, courtesy of Charlie.

Emma Blackwell snuggled closer to her husband, Justin, on one of the couches, glancing around the room, her heart filled with love as she took in her family.

Hunter and Rina lay curled up together on one of the couches, arms around each other, watching *It's A Wonderful Life.*

Billy, Rina's nephew whom they'd adopted when his parents were killed, lay sprawled in front of the TV, shoveling handfuls of popcorn into his mouth as he watched the old black and white movie, mesmerized.

Colt and Brenna sat on another couch, arms around each other, pretending to watch the movie, but they were really just watching each other.

Cutter and Sara were pacing around the room, arm in arm, laughing, talking softly, trying to walk off a cramp Sara had developed after dinner.

Endy and Sadie were snoring quietly on one of the couches.

"Do you believe this, Em?" Justin Blackwell whispered in his wife's ear. "This is our family. *Our* children and *our* grandchildren." His voice held such pride Emma wanted to weep, remembering the days, so long ago when they thought they'd never have a child, let alone a family.

"I do, honey." She snuggled closer. Although age had whitened their hair, and lined their faces, nothing—nothing had diminished the love or desire they'd felt the moment they'd laid eyes on one another.

"And would you look at Colt?" Justin grinned. "Sitting there right near the Christmas tree watching an old Christmas movie." He shook his head. "I never thought we'd ever see it."

"Me neither," Emma whispered, lifting a hand to her husband's cheek. "I always told you that love could work miracles." She turned his face for a kiss. "Didn't I?"

Justin laughed, running a hand lovingly up her back. "I've never doubted anything you've ever told me, hon, not in all these forty wonderful years."

"Colt," Brenna said sleepily. "Did you enjoy Christmas?" She held her breath, waiting. This was so important to him, to her, to all of them.

He grinned. "Yeah, you're right. I'd forgotten how much fun Christmas was." He drew her into the circle of his arms. "Especially with kids."

"Colt?" She frowned, remembering something he'd said, or rather something she saw, on Charlie's brand-new red Christmas nightgown. "What happened to the sheriff's badge you bought for your brother?"

He grinned. "I gave it to Charlie. This afternoon."

"You gave it to—Oh Colt." She threw her arms around him for a hug.

"It seemed fitting somehow, that she should have it. It's because of her, and you, that all of this happened. I'll never forget Cade, not ever, but because of you and Charlie and the rest of the kids, I can finally put it rest. Instead of being a symbol of the past, now that badge is a symbol of the future. Our future." Colt glanced around the room, and felt the love.

His mother and father.

His brother Hunter and Rina.

His brother Cutter and his sister Sara. And their babies to be.

Brenna, his beautiful Brenna.

And the kids.

His kids. His family.

As Colt Blackwell sat in the middle of the room, surrounded by family, surrounded by love, surrounded by the spirit of Christmas once again, that part of him, the small, fragile part of the eight-year-old boy's scarred, wounded heart slowly, finally began to heal.

In that instant, Colt Blackwell finally forgave himself for something he'd been too young to control. And with forgiveness, came peace, blissful peace at last, and the knowledge that he could and would…love.

* * * * *

SILHOUETTE'S 20TH ANNIVERSARY CONTEST
OFFICIAL RULES
NO PURCHASE NECESSARY TO ENTER

1. To enter, follow directions published in the offer to which you are responding. Contest begins 1/1/00 and ends on 8/24/00 (the "Promotion Period"). Method of entry may vary. Mailed entries must be postmarked by 8/24/00, and received by 8/31/00.

2. During the Promotion Period, the Contest may be presented via the Internet. Entry via the Internet may be restricted to residents of certain geographic areas that are disclosed on the Web site. To enter via the Internet, if you are a resident of a geographic area in which Internet entry is permissible, follow the directions displayed on-line, including typing your essay of 100 words or fewer telling us "Where In The World Your Love Will Come Alive." On-line entries must be received by 11:59 p.m. Eastern Standard time on 8/24/00. Limit one e-mail entry per person, household and e-mail address per day, per presentation. If you are a resident of a geographic area in which entry via the Internet is permissible, you may, in lieu of submitting an entry on-line, enter by mail, by hand-printing your name, address, telephone number and contest number/name on an 8"x 11" plain piece of paper and telling us in 100 words or fewer "Where In The World Your Love Will Come Alive," and mailing via first-class mail to: Silhouette 20th Anniversary Contest, (in the U.S.) P.O. Box 9069, Buffalo, NY 14269-9069; (In Canada) P.O. Box 637, Fort Erie, Ontario, Canada L2A 5X3. Limit one 8"x 11" mailed entry per person, household and e-mail address per day. <u>On-line and/or 8"x 11" mailed entries received from persons residing in geographic areas in which Internet entry is not permissible will be disqualified.</u> No liability is assumed for lost, late, incomplete, inaccurate, nondelivered or misdirected mail, or misdirected e-mail, for technical, hardware or software failures of any kind, lost or unavailable network connection, or failed, incomplete, garbled or delayed computer transmission or any human error which may occur in the receipt or processing of the entries in the contest.

3. Essays will be judged by a panel of members of the Silhouette editorial and marketing staff based on the following criteria:

   Sincerity (believability, credibility)—50%
   Originality (freshness, creativity)—30%
   Aptness (appropriateness to contest ideas)—20%

   Purchase or acceptance of a product offer does not improve your chances of winning. In the event of a tie, duplicate prizes will be awarded.

4. All entries become the property of Harlequin Enterprises Ltd., and will not be returned. Winner will be determined no later than 10/31/00 and will be notified by mail. Grand Prize winner will be required to sign and return Affidavit of Eligibility within 15 days of receipt of notification. Noncompliance within the time period may result in disqualification and an alternative winner may be selected. All municipal, provincial, federal, state and local laws and regulations apply. Contest open only to residents of the U.S. and Canada who are 18 years of age or older, and is void wherever prohibited by law. Internet entry is restricted solely to residents of those geographical areas in which Internet entry is permissible. Employees of Torstar Corp., their affiliates, agents and members of their immediate families are not eligible. Taxes on the prizes are the sole responsibility of winners. Entry and acceptance of any prize offered constitutes permission to use winner's name, photograph or other likeness for the purposes of advertising, trade and promotion on behalf of Torstar Corp. without further compensation to the winner, unless prohibited by law. Torstar Corp and D.L. Blair, Inc., their parents, affiliates and subsidiaries, are not responsible for errors in printing or electronic presentation of contest or entries. In the event of printing or other errors which may result in unintended prize values or duplication of prizes, all affected contest materials or entries shall be null and void. If for any reason the Internet portion of the contest is not capable of running as planned, including infection by computer virus, bugs, tampering, unauthorized intervention, fraud, technical failures, or any other causes beyond the control of Torstar Corp. which corrupt or affect the administration, secrecy, fairness, integrity or proper conduct of the contest, Torstar Corp. reserves the right, at its sole discretion, to disqualify any individual who tampers with the entry process and to cancel, terminate, modify or suspend the contest or the Internet portion thereof. In the event of a dispute regarding an on-line entry, the entry will be deemed submitted by the authorized holder of the e-mail account submitted at the time of entry. Authorized account holder is defined as the natural person who is assigned to an e-mail address by an Internet access provider, on-line service provider or other organization that is responsible for arranging e-mail address for the domain associated with the submitted e-mail address.

5. Prizes: Grand Prize—a $10,000 vacation to anywhere in the world. Travelers (at least one must be 18 years of age or older) or parent or guardian if one traveler is a minor, must sign and return a Release of Liability prior to departure. Travel must be completed by December 31, 2001, and is subject to space and accommodations availability. Two hundred (200) Second Prizes—a two-book limited edition autographed collector set from one of the Silhouette Anniversary authors: Nora Roberts, Diana Palmer, Linda Howard or Annette Broadrick (value $10.00 each set). All prizes are valued in U.S. dollars.

6. For a list of winners (available after 10/31/00), send a self-addressed, stamped envelope to: Harlequin Silhouette 20th Anniversary Winners, P.O. Box 4200, Blair, NE 68009-4200.

Contest sponsored by Torstar Corp., P.O. Box 9042, Buffalo, NY 14269-9042.